You have g
to see this

Shari Bera

WORK LOG

Aaaaaaaaaaaaaahhhhhhhhhhhhh. Not all soil is the same and I am currently standing on some that you can sink up to your knees in. I step over here, nope, not any better. Sometimes I have to remind myself why I am doing this, I mean I could have a cozy office job in the Apple. And I wonder who decided to name the city "Apple". I read somewhere that there used to be a city nicknamed The Big Apple, but I would have to check the GPS coordinates to see how close our city is to where that city was. But I digress, it is so easy to let my mind wander off when I am on assignment out here searching for a lost item. I am an archaeological retrieval agent and I work for the government. I try to take one more step and find that I stepped on something hard. I reach down and start digging around near my foot. Ah-ha! This is what I was looking for. Sometimes I think I am more lucky than skilled but whatever gets the job done. I finish digging it up, fill out the form and head back to the city.

My job is quite simple. I am given either landmarks or approximate locations to go search for things that the government thinks are valuable or could be valuable that might have survived the Great War. My first year was spent as an understudy to one of the best retrieval agents in my department. She could calculate any distance based on the littlest information. She could triangulate any coordinates and come up with the object in question even when some of the coordinates were smudged or smeared. I looked up to her and tried to learn everything I could from her in that first year. If I ever had any questions or needed help, she would never give me the answer right away. She would help me work through it to find the answer. She was the best teacher or mentor that I have ever had because she made me think for myself. Now there were instances after that first year where I needed her help with a problem that I had not encountered before and she would always help me work through the options until I found a solution.

But one day, she did not show up to work. I remember the commotion as all of the top bosses came down and asked everyone to tell them if she said anything or alluded to why she was missing. Apparently, they checked her abode and she was not anywhere to be found. It is like she disappeared overnight. I was sad but did not want anyone to know how much I admired her. Personal relationships are discouraged between people of different ranks and she outranked me. So, I never told anyone how much of an impact she had on me. No one would understand. Sometimes my coworkers will compare my talents to hers, but in those words. They do not want to admit that she left and so they say my talents are similar to hers. Part of the mystery is that she did not leave any kind of communication that she was leaving, she simply disappeared and no one knows why. She is still missing. I assume she is still alive because in the city there is no violence and no violent crimes like the ancestors had. For example, I can assume that she was not murdered. But it is still a mystery that I think about from time to time.

I have been sent on retrieval missions with groups of coworkers and I have been sent alone. Sometimes it takes a group to find a small object and sometimes it takes a group to haul a large object back to the department. One time I was in a group that was sent to find this monument that was shaped like an obelisk. It was named after a person or a place, I cannot remember but the government expected to find it in large pieces. Instead it was in about two feet sections. It was so important that one of the top bosses went with my group to oversee the retrieval. When it was found to be in small pieces, we were instructed to try to put it back together like a puzzle while he called in the results of our find to his bosses. It was not a pleasant communication, all of us could tell this from his end of the communication. When we returned to the office, the archives department helped us reassemble as much of the monument as we could in the museum.

We have this large museum dedicated to the ancestors in the timeline which we think they lived. It helps school children in their history classes and it helps adults to stay within the constraints of the government. It is like a big example of this is what the ancestors did and since their world ended in a Great War that destroyed everything in their way of life, you should not do this and you should trust your government. Since we are constantly updating the artifacts and the timeline, school children and adults are made to visit and revisit the museum regularly. If we have found something large or made a large discovery that rearranges the timeline, then everyone has to come back shortly after the discovery is made. Usually, a citizen will get a communication that says on Wednesday after work, you may visit the museum. The government knows which jobs are demanding and when, so they schedule your visit for you. I have seen different groups come through in this manner. I have never received this type of communication because I work at the museum and know everything in it. I have also worked at some of the showings so if anyone has any questions, I can help explain what the object was or what its purpose was. There is always a government approved write up about the new objects but some people need a little more help understanding these things so there are always retrieval agents and archive department employees around.

Today I am being sent out to find an object on a single mission, which is what I usually do. I have been given very little information from my bosses. I try to calculate the coordinates but there is just not enough information. I speak to a couple of coworkers to see if they have had this little of information before but no one can help me. I really wish my mentor was around because she could solve this problem. I go through every problem-solving technique I know and I come up with different answers every time. In this case, the object is referenced by another object that must have been well known to the ancestors but has long been lost to my generation. I try to work out the exact location of the referenced object from our archives but I cannot figure that out either. It seems quite frustrating that there is not a better way to do this. I take what I can from the information that was given to me and decide to just go fly around in the area and see if I can find any more information. I know this object was in the flood area but not the fire area so I am going to look in the part of the country that used to be Northwestern Pennsylvania. In this area there were dams and some large lakes that were targeted by other countries to create havoc and mayhem. Because there is so much water everywhere in this area, the bombs did not create widespread fires, like in the western part of the country.

I sign out my flying apparatus for additional time to search. Some bosses expect their employees to sign out and sign in with more detail but I am usually given more freedom because I take on the hardest cases. Since I don't want to cause any concern, I sign it out this time with the case number so everyone knows what I am looking for and how long I think this search will take. The first time a case is worked, it is given an original case number which is all numbers. If it is not solved, it receives another case designator which is a letter. The case number keeps evolving in this fashion so the longer the case number, the more it has been worked on and not solved.

I leave and head out of the city. My first of five different coordinates take me to a hillside that mostly survived the flood because of its location and elevation. Most of the water just simply flowed around the hill. I park my flying apparatus and search with a metal detector. Nothing, not even one beep. Okay, off to the second set of coordinates. No, this location does not match the description at all. Come on lucky number three. This third set of coordinates places me at a location that has some of the physical attributes, there is a river, there is a hill, but no area that could have been a pond or a lake. As I am flying to the fourth set of coordinates, I think I catch some movement in my peripheral but when I move my head and slow my flight, nothing moves again. Well, that was weird. Anyway, off to the fourth set of coordinates. This one has as much potential as the first one did so I get out and check with the metal detector. Nothing, nothing, beep. Great! I grab my shovel and dig about two feet down. I hit this little black box and dig it up. This is not the object I am looking for but it is quite interesting. There is a couple of knobs, one moves a white line along an area that has numbers on the top and bottom. One line is labeled AM and one is labeled FM. I have no idea what this contraption is but I decide to take it along and put it with my treasures. It also has some other labels on it and I think I can research what it was. There is an electrical cord and I have to see if I can find my adapter. Back in the ancestors' time, many devices had this cord to transfer energy to the device to make it work. Today we use solar power for everything, no need for cords. So archaic, really. Also, all devices now are made to get charged during the hours the sun is available but efficient so that during the non-sun hours, they still hold their charge. I read that once you unplugged these devices from their power source, they stopped working. But I put this device into a compartment on my flying apparatus and search the area again with the metal detector. Nothing else causes a beep so I am off to the fifth location. Well this does not meet the criteria either. I don't see any other possible locations in the area that meets the description with a river, a hill and a pond so I slowly fly a different route back to the office, looking for a place that matches the description. Maybe I will have some luck and just happen upon it. Wait, what is that over there? There is definitely a hill and a river beside it. Let me just fly a little closer to see if I can find an area that could have been a pond. Oooh, there is a depression in the ground just big enough to have collected water. I fly back to the hilltop and pull out my metal detector. I make some sweeps over here, some sweeps over there, I go a little further this way, I go a little further that way until I hear a blip. This blip means there is something close to the surface and not too large. Again, it's not what I am looking for but it could be a treasure. I find several coins in a scattered pile. The floods brought them here and deposited some soil on top of them. It's not a big enough pile that anyone would be looking for so I put them into my pocket and keep them. These will go into my treasure room at my abode. By the time I get back to my flying apparatus, it is quite late and I decide to just fly to my abode instead of back to the office.

Once I arrive at my abode, I unload my treasures and make myself some dinner. Today is Thursday so I make the Thursday portion of food from the food pellets. I am feeling frustrated that I could not find my object today and start to think about ways to improve my calculations to be able to find it later. That just makes me more frustrated. I think instead I will look up my new treasures. I have found that if I research them shortly after I get home, it is still interesting. If I wait too long after I get home and have a backlog to investigate, then it seems like work. So this first treasure, the black box, is called a radio and it is made to listen to music. I plug the cord into my adapter and charge it. There is no sound. My research tells me that on the AM and FM sections, there should be channels so I move the knob to scan through these channels. I hear some static but no music. If this played music from the ancestors age, I wonder what it would be like. I can do all kinds of research into music but it only results in information about artists and genres, nothing actually has music. The government approved music of today is just an arranged set of beeps, blips and the like. There are no voices and no rhythm. The government claims that music from the past led to riots, violence and started an uprising against the government so it was banned. I researched the ancestors' music for a history class but the professor said the topic was not appropriate to learn about and chose a different topic for me. It seemed odd at the time but I did not want to cause any trouble so I researched a new topic.

The coins are easy to research because they have so much info on each one. I see that I have found two quarters, five dimes and twelve pennies. This idea of paying for things is so different than what we do now. The government provides you what you need. You get a monthly ration of food, specified by day. You get all the personal items you need based on your personal dynamics, age, sex, height and weight. This is the only way I have ever known how to live. I get a glimpse of how the ancestors lived and I try to imagine what it was like but I see how our way of life is better now that the government controls everything. There is simply no violence and no crime. Everyone and everything have its place and the system runs smoothly. You do not even have to worry about what clothes to wear or if someone has nicer clothes than you because everyone wears a uniform based on their job. All of the archaeological retrieval agents wear a specific uniform but it is different than the uniforms of nurses which is different than the uniforms of the agents in the archives department and so on.

TREASURE LOG

I have accumulated some treasures along my career as a retrieval agent. Some of these items may not seem to be important to other people and I know most of my coworkers would never think about bringing items back from a dig site to their abode but I find some of these things quite interesting. I really enjoyed my history classes and learning about what our ancestors did with these objects. I do not have many items but I have some great little finds. Sometimes if I cannot find what the original purpose was, I imagine what these objects could have been used for.

One of my first treasures is still a mystery. It measures approximately 9 inches by 12 inches. It is made of plastic, like so many things from the ancestors' age. It is clear and has rows of puffed rectangles of packaged air. My research has netted no definitive results. I wonder if this was the fancy air. One of these puffed rectangles burst and made an incredible popping noise. But I smelled the air and it did not seem any different than normal air. Normally we usually can only find things that will set off the metal detector but as I was digging for something else, I saw a corner of this plastic thing. Most plastic things are kind of boring but this little mystery caught my attention.

Another one of my little treasures was found the same way. It is a little plastic toy. I cannot seem to figure out its purpose but it says "made for McDonalds" on it. While doing research on this toy, I came across an interesting fact that even though this McDonalds was a food place, it distributed these little toys.

Again this is something that we were not sent to retrieve but as I was digging up something else, I found it.

I came across some jewelry on a trip that I thought was a treasure. I found a necklace, some bracelets, a couple rings and some decorated pins. I cleaned them up when I got them home and researched them. I am sure they are not valuable but I liked them so I brought them back to my abode. I try to think of what kind of girl would have worn this jewelry. What was her life like that she would have liked this type of necklace? Some of my questions I will never know the answer to but I still like to think about them.

I also have what the ancestors called a cell phone. One side is cracked and without a power cord, this is another example of something that we have found but do not know how it worked. There is not an example of a cell phone anywhere that I know of that survived the Great War in a good working condition. Most of the ones we have are damaged but so far, we have not been able to get one to work. We were able to find one with a power cord, but once we plugged in our adapter, the only thing we could get was a password screen. I decided to bring this one to my abode because it had an outer case that I liked. We have seen a few examples of these cell phones and we have been able to pull some of the outer cases off, but I liked this one, so I kept it.

GROUP SEARCH LOG

Today I was sent out on a mission with a group of coworkers to find a large landmark that was a well-known waterfall. This would normally be easy to find but with the earthquakes, the bombs and the flooding that occurred in this area, the landscape changed dramatically from how the ancestors used to know it. This waterfall was known to be on the border of two countries and was in the area that was known as New York State. We head to where the coordinates lead us and land the group flying apparatus. The group scatters in different directions. We work for close to an hour testing the ground for different soil composition that would indicate a large river flowed through at one time. We probe the ground to see if there are any soft spots indicating new soil landed on top of hard packed soil. Another hour later and we seem to be narrowing down and closing in on our targeted waterfalls.

There is a loud screeching noise all of a sudden that sounds like it is coming out of the sky. Everyone stops what they are doing to find out what is making the noise. An ancient satellite comes streaking across the sky and lands within a half a mile from our location. I start to walk over to it because ancient satellites often carry info about the ancestors past inside them. Some of the crew members come with me to check out the crash site. When something of this size makes an impact, many times the soil will be disturbed and you can find clues that you might have missed before. Possibly even clues that will lead to the river bed or the waterfalls.

Once we arrive at the crash site, the crew scatters again, some looking for soil samples, some looking at the water content of the disturbed soil, but I head directly to the satellite. The way that each person heads is a great indication of their strength in our department. The ones looking at the soil samples really bring a different set of knowledge points to this case than I do. Even if I were to find something different in the soil, I would have no idea what it would mean. The satellite has some markings on it that indicate it was a radio satellite with a call sign of a radio station and some numbers. I take a couple of pictures to analyze later. I open panels in order to access the inside of the satellite. There are instructions and a repair manual. Well, I hardly think it can be repaired any longer so I fold both of these up and put them in my carrying sack. I check with my coworkers but no one has found anything significant. We decide to head back to the location where we were before the satellite crashed. I have seen a few satellite crashes when I am out on a mission. The ancestors had plenty of satellites orbiting the planet and their life span happens to be ending so I expect more to fall out of the sky.

One of my coworkers has detected large boulders that are buried very close to each other. This could be the bottom of the waterfalls. We check a couple more details from the original information we were given and determine that this is the location of the waterfalls. We document all of the data, the GPS coordinates and the location of the boulders. We usually do all of the documenting before leaving the site in case we forget to collect a certain piece of data. The form we fill out is quite comprehensive and it would be easy to forget a section of it if we were to fill it out at the office. Niagara was the name of the waterfall but I will have to check why it was named that.

We fly back to the office because we have accomplished today's mission. The bosses are happy we found this location even if there was not anything to retrieve from that location. It is one of the landmarks that we can now use as reference points when trying to find either other landmarks or other retrieval sites. I help document the GPS coordinates for the waterfalls named Niagara and load as much info as I can into the database from the form we filled out earlier. This should aid the next researcher who might need this information.

When I get home, I unpack my new treasures. Most of the paper was destroyed in the Great War either from the fires or the bombs. There are not any more paper making factories since the government determined that it was a wasteful and inefficient form of communication. I value any and all paper that I find. I make my Tuesday portion of my dinner and eat while reading through the instruction manual from the satellite. It has multiple languages. I read through some schematics and then I find what I am looking for, the purpose of the satellite. It says it was for sending out radio waves for radio stations and this satellite was specifically for what the ancestors called SiriusXM radio. There are some numbers that must represent the different radio stations.

I think I have a radio in my treasure room. I go find it, plug it into the power adapter and start putting the dial on these different numbers. Nothing, nothing, there is something here on this one. It is so slight that it does not surprise me that I missed it in my original search with this dial. I need something that will boost the signal to this radio so I can pick up the radio wave clearer. I have a device I use on my retrieval trips when I am far across the country and need to send info back to the office. I wonder if that will boost this signal as well. I go find it and attach it to the radio and out comes what I imagine is called music. "I can see clearly now the rain is gone. I can see all obstacles in my way." The tune is amazing, I could listen to this all day. I turn the volume up a little and sit and enjoy my new found music. Each new song makes me smile more and more until I realize just how much I really love this new treasure. I make a mark on the radio scale and try to move down the dial. With this signal booster I find a couple more radio stations, marking each one as I go along. "May I have your attention, please? Will the real Slim Shady please stand up?" Oh, on this station the songs are being spoken quickly. I really have to listen intently but it seems like the person speaking is very good because he speaks really fast all the while he rhymes his lyrics.

"It was a clear black night, a clear white moon Warren G is on the streets, trying to consume some skirts for the eve, so I can get some funk." I am not sure what some of these phrases mean but I find myself trying to say the words in my mind after the songs are over. This type of music is great. I really do not understand why the government would have this music banned. Listening to it does not make me want to cause harm to others. Music cannot incite violence; it cannot cause people to create havoc.

SINGLE MISSION LOG

Typically, I spend three days in the office doing research on a future mission, planning it out, calculating coordinates and plotting a flight path or following up on research on a past mission, documenting what was found, where it was found, the exact GPS coordinates and logging it into the databases. But two days a week I go on retrieval trips. When I first started, I enjoyed the office work and was a little scared of the singular retrieval trips. I have grown up with the assumption that whatever is outside of the Apple is not worth my time and possibly dangerous. The government, through the media, is constantly discouraging its citizens from leaving the Apple. We are really controlled through the media and no one questions the motive because the government wants us all to live in peace and to be happy and productive. The ancestors messed up everything because they did not have this control in place.

I still like to spend my time researching but sometimes I find it easier to research from home on any topic that I do not want to share with my coworkers. But I feel like now, I am starting to really enjoy my time on the single mission trips. I like to be alone on a trip, and I like to be alone researching in my abode.

The cases that we receive are mostly delegated to us from our supervisors, usually based on past performance on similar missions. We have the option of volunteering for some missions in the section of harder cases or the ones that an agent could not find. Some of my coworkers do not like to fly their apparatus by themselves and are sent out in a double or only in group missions. Some of my coworkers are still learning and they are paired up with retrieval agent mentors, like I was in the beginning. We have more individuality in my department because a large part of our job is based on individual talent. We aren't given many freedoms within this new government but having a talent will allow you a little more freedom to use your talent naturally. I guess the government understands that if you told a fish to climb a tree, it would spend its life thinking it was stupid. The government uses this quote to push the citizens into finding the best job for them. It really helps to keep everyone happy in their job and happiness leads to a peaceful society.

One of my first solo retrieval trips was a long distance one. I had to get to a location in the southwest part of the country where there were large fires. The landscape here is different from the areas near the Apple. Because it takes longer to get here, you have to be more precise in your calculations but once you get here, the object can be easier to find because you only have to search through ash, not ash and river mud and bomb displaced debris. I wish there was an easier way to get here because I would like to spend some time exploring this area, in my flying apparatus and by walking around. But the first trip was a nice one. I found the location easily and parked my apparatus. There was a stash of obsidian points that were made by some of the earliest settlers in the country. These points were made of obsidian rocks that the people would sharpen and tie to sticks in order to kill animals. I really enjoy learning how these other people lived because it shows how different people were. I think these people were the ancestors to the ancestors. I documented the site and brought back several items for the museum to display. Because I had found the location easily and the objects easily, I took my time returning to the office. I did not see the trouble, the violence or the beasts that the government claimed would be out here. I wondered why the government would play all of those ads discouraging people to come out here when there was not any danger that I could see. Maybe I went to the safe part of the country and I just did not see the parts that the government was talking about.

Another one of my first trips was to find what was called tools. I worked the calculations, flew to the site and started looking for these objects. The metal detector is quiet for a long time until I hear the first beep. I look back at how far away I am from where I thought it was going to be. Hmmmm. It seems like I just wasted about thirty minutes trying to find the right spot. I start digging up the area and find multiple different items. I researched what these tools were before I came out here. Well, I researched as much as I could, there was not a lot of info on the individual tools. But I know most of their names. I was sent here to look for examples of screwdrivers, hammers, and wrenches. I was also sent to find their corresponding counterparts like screws, nails, nuts and bolts. I find other tools that have the electrical cord attached but since these were not requested for this trip, I leave them here. I do pick them up, clean the dirt off and turn them over in my hands. I try to figure out what they would have been used for. Without seeing them work, sometimes it is hard to figure out what part would have required the electricity and what its special purpose would have been. There are two types of screwdrivers, one with a flat line and one with a cross top. And there are all sizes of screwdrivers, from small to large. I do not know why there had to be so many different options. It seems like it would have been easier if the ancestors' government had regulated that. If there was only one choice, things would have been better. I think the same would have been true for the wrenches. There are so many different sizes. I grab the tools that I was instructed to retrieve and fill out my form. I add details about the other tools I have found and put down the exact location just in case they decide that the other tools are important enough to retrieve.

RESEARCH LOG

When I first started my career as a retrieval agent, after all of my proper education and training, I was often given little test assignments to see what areas I would be the best at. Some agents are better at research in the office while others are better at the retrieval missions. Some agents are given the opportunity to move into a supervisor role after a few years of office work also. When I was given the research mini tests, I often excelled but I have more of a talent for the retrieval missions. And I really like my job as it is now. I do not have the desire to be a supervisor because I would rather be in charge of objects than people.

There was one of these research tests that I recall with great detail. I had to search through the archives to see the previously successful location mission trips. I had to find in the archives the section where the Grand Canyon was relocated and documented. The Grand Canyon is in an area of the country that was devastated by large fires so many of the landmarks are easy to find. You read the description and imagine the place without any living vegetation. The Grand Canyon is a large opening in the landscape so it was one of the first places that my department was able to find. They had to work out what to find and what to do with the information once it was found. After a few missions, the form we fill out now was initiated. So now there is a section to put as much information as might be needed. The logic was to start with something easy, take as much data as possible and return to the office and see what was actually needed for a documentation to start recording history again in the archives. I read all of the documentation and thought about how exciting it must have been for those involved. They were flying a group transport and they happened to fly right over it. It must have looked so spectacular from above. I also note that their calculations for this location were not quite right, which is why they flew over it the first time.

After I read about this first find, I continued to research what other landmarks were documented in the first days of the retrieval department. They did not retrieve anything but they were still known as the retrieval department. Maybe they should have been known as the Archaeology Department instead. Who knows? One of the next missions was a man-made object but it was well known in the ancestors' time. It was called the Golden Gate Bridge, even though it was an orange color. Sometimes I just cannot understand the naming convention behind some of the objects. In this case, bridge is the only accurate part of the name. But as I read the documentation and looked at the pictures, this bridge was a massive object that the ancestors made. Many subsequent mission trips in this area were based off the location of this bridge. The calculations from the first mission were off but as the team got closer, they could easily find the landmark. This bridge and the next landmark were built sturdy enough to withstand the fires and the following floods because they were made very well. The Seattle Space Needle is another landmark that was used in following missions as a key landmark. It is also another object that I just don't quite understand the name, Space Needle. What is a space needle? It was not tall enough to reach into space. It is not used as a needle. This landmark intrigues me, I think I want to find out more about it.

These were easy to identify and document as the department grew. There are still mystery finds that have been located but not identified. Sometimes when these mystery objects were found, they were categorized as a mystery and are still labeled as such. At different times, each agent is scheduled time to work on these mysteries and many different agents leave notes on what they think the purpose could have been. Some people will enter an argument as to why it could or could not be the purpose. For example, there is this one mystery that has baffled many of my coworkers. There are these tall metal towers connected by some metal cables. Hanging from these cables are bench seats of varying sizes. These tower and chair combos are located in different areas of the country but usually on mountains. Not all mountains have them while some mountains have multiple towers. Why would the ancestors need to ride a bench seat from the top of the mountain down to the bottom? Why are they different sizes, like some look like they fit two people and others look to fit as many as six. Plus, these bench seats are often pretty high in the air, especially in the middle. Did they ride in the full circle or down and then back up? So confusing. As with other man-made objects, some are still standing while others have started falling down. Some of the materials that these things were made of did not last very long before they started deteriorating. Sometimes pieces have fallen apart. There are examples of these towers where the cable has deteriorated and the bench seats are on the ground. Some towers have fallen over and the whole system is on the ground and in some areas the whole system is still standing. In some places you can tell that the environment caused the destruction while in other places the destruction was directly caused by the Great War.

On one of my early retrieval test trips I was sent with my mentor to see one of these metal seat towers. She walked me through calculating the coordinates of three different sites. One site was still standing, one site was on the ground and the third site was half still standing and half on the ground. She wanted to see what kind of theories I could come up with for the purpose of these seat systems. After surveying all three sites and after looking at them from all angles and trying to imagine what they were for, I simply asked her one question, what if the ancestors were riding up the mountain instead of down? She said that the general consensus is that the ancestors went down the mountain or for a full circle ride. What made me think that the ancestors would want to ride up the mountain? We had parked our flying apparatus at a spot around the middle of the mountain and I asked her to hike with me partially up the mountain and then partially down the mountain. I asked her which direction she would prefer to ride. She said up. I said point proven. Maybe not every problem can be solved in the office, maybe sometimes you have to go to the place, get the feel of the place, see the sights and smell the smells. I did not think about how hard it would be to walk up or down this mountain until we arrived here and started walking. There is quite the difference.

After proving that I was good at the retrieval trips, I requested to go to the Seattle Space Needle on a retrieval mission.

Sometimes we can go to a place and just search around to see what we find. I plotted the course and because the trip was a long one, I requested an overnight stay so I took one of the enclosed flying apparatus so I could sleep in it. I arrived at the site pretty late in the day so I just walked around and looked at the Space Needle from different angles. This is an interesting building and seeing it in person really makes you appreciate its size. I head back to the flying apparatus and get ready to sleep. This was my first overnight trip but I have heard from some of my coworkers that they are not as scary as you would think. After the Great War, the wildlife was decimated and all of the people now live in the city. There is nothing out here. Again, I question the advertisements that the government play saying that there is violence and beasts outside of the city. My coworkers will not discuss theories but they will state facts. And the fact that none of them have ever seen any beasts is something they will not tell anyone outside of the department. They do not want to contradict what the government has said.

The next day I wake up and eat my morning food rations and start my day. It is not until I eat my morning food that I realize I was so excited for this trip that I did not eat any dinner food. I take the metal detector and am surprised just how many hits I am getting in this area. Some are close to the surface and I dig them up easily. I find coins, nails, screws and small circular objects that are the size of coins but have ridges around the sides. I fan out and work in a larger grid pattern. I realize I have been working for a while and decide to stop and eat my lunch rations. I also think that it is starting to get late in the day and I need to leave soon to get back across the country to the city. But then, interrupting my thoughts, is a large long beep. Ooohhh, something large, metal and close to the surface. I get a digging tool out of my flying apparatus and start digging until I hit the object. I dig around the sides, and then I dig down to the bottom until I can finally move it from its resting place. This is a large green metal trunk and it is heavy. There is not any type of lock in the latch so I open it easily. To my amazement, it is filled with books, like real books made of paper. I read about these in the archives but this is the first time I have seen a real book made of paper.

The book on top is a large colorful book with many pictures. The title states that it is of national treasures. I flip through a couple pages and it shows the Grand Canyon and the Golden Gate Bridge. This will be valuable to the archives. Imagine having pictures and descriptions of these places written by the ancestors. We will know for sure what the purpose and significance of some of the landmarks were to them. How exciting! I notice that there are objects in this book that my department has not found yet. The supervisors are going to love this new treasure. There is also a large colorful book of world landmarks. There are plenty of books in this trunk but for now I have to load it up and start on my return trip. This trunk is quite heavy so I decide to bring my flying apparatus closer instead of trying to drag this trunk all the way over to the apparatus. I strap the trunk to the apparatus and fly back to my abode. I will take the trunk of books into the office tomorrow.

The next day I haul the trunk into the office and straight to the archives. I check the flying apparatus back in and to my surprise, no one says anything to me about the fact that I went to my abode last night and did not return from my trip with enough time to come to the office. That is interesting. I add all of my data about the find into the archives and take the books in to be catalogued. These books will now be available to all the agents in my department as well as the other similar departments like the history one and the archives one. We work closely with a few different departments and I really enjoy sharing information with these other departments. We are often encouraged to collaborate with these other departments because it usually results in some excellent new finds.

I have been back several times to look at these books. If I do not have any active retrieval cases that I am working on, I will go and read these books or see what updates have been made to the archives. The world landmarks book shows pictures of things that I did not know existed. I now have read about the Great Wall of China, the Great Pyramids of Giza and the Sphinx, the Leaning Tower of Pisa, and the waterways in the city of Venice. There are so many great works done by the ancestors and maybe done by their ancestors. I wonder what it would have been like to live in that time before most of these things were destroyed. I can imagine standing at the base of the Great Wall of China and being amazed at its height just as I was amazed standing at the base of the Seattle Space Needle. I can imagine standing on a bridge in the city of Venice and watching the gondola boats below me. I wonder if the ancestors appreciated these landmarks or if they were so used to them that it was normal to see a leaning tower on your way to work.

While exploring different sites in the southwestern part of the country, I was sent to one of the larger city sites. Seeing these large cities in the southwest where the country only experienced fires, is very eerie. There are just large areas of abandoned buildings. Most of these cities had rectangular multi storied buildings. But this city was different, there were large buildings but there was one with a pirate ship and one looked like it had a roller coaster around it. There was also one that was a pyramid and had a sphinx in front of it. If I had not been reading and rereading the books I found, I would have been impressed with these two buildings. I realize that these buildings are replicas of real places. I will add that fact to the archives. This city built replicas of other places. I wonder what the point of that was. Why would you make a replica city? I wonder if it was also named the Replica City? Knowing the ancestors, it's name probably had nothing to do with the replicas.

PROBLEM WITH THE CALCULATIONS

It has really been a concern of mine that our calculations just are not correct. It seems like we are close. I start to think there has to be a better way to do this. Sometimes the information we get is incomplete and there just is no improving on that. I assume the bosses give the supervisors all the information we will need for the retrieval trip that they have. It just seems like maybe there is a way to make our calculations more accurate. I do not have any important cases today so I decide I am going to sit down and try to figure this out. I look at the Grand Canyon trip. Since this was the first trip made by my department, there is actually a lot of information in this file. In the file it shows the information they originally had and the way they worked their calculations. That all seems correct, it is the same as we do our calculations now. But then I look at the actual coordinates and see if maybe I can work the calculations backwards. Hmmm, it seems like it should work. I cannot quite figure out why it does not work. I work at it for a couple more hours and then it is time to leave for the day. How frustrating that I could not get it to work. It seems like somewhere I have learned how to work through problems like this. But today I cannot seem to remember how to solve this type of problem. There are times where I feel like I am getting close to solving a problem and then my brain gets tired and I just cannot seem to work any longer that day. I think that my concentration has deteriorated over the years. I do not remember this being a problem while I was in school or when I was interning.

GROUP MISSION LOG

Sometimes I am sent on group missions when there is a large object to find. Not all missions given to us as a group make sense to me, I do not know why we are looking for such things. We are going today on such a group mission with about twenty of my coworkers including myself and three supervisors. It seems a little excessive but what do I know, I am just a worker. The announcement of who was going on this trip was made fifteen minutes before departure so I am completely unprepared for this retrieval assignment, as are all of my coworkers. We are briefed in the large transport flying apparatus on the way to the site. While they are assigning tasks, I look around at my coworkers. Whoever put together this team did a good job because the tasks are assigned to the people who are strong in those tasks. I know all of my coworkers but one of the supervisors must be new because I do not remember seeing him around the office at all. We will be looking for a large building with multiple interior walls. We need to officially locate the building, document the GPS coordinates and set up a scan of the entire location. Apparently, there will be no retrieving of anything at this site, so it is for locational analysis only, which is odd. We normally don't need this many agents for a location mission trip.

Once we land, it is apparent that we are at the location. There are subtle clues from the surrounding area. There is a definite increase in ground height in a rectangular area. The supervisors are busy plotting the initial GPS coordinates at each of the main outside points. My coworkers and I set up the ground penetrating laser radar system. This system involves an unmanned flying drone that scans the ground in a grid pattern then transmits all that data to an on-site processor and also to a processor back at the office. When the drone is in the air, we grab handheld scanners to start looking at outlying areas. You never know for sure what areas were hit by bombs in the Great War and if a bomb hit here, it could have scattered debris outside of the building's perimeter. Again, I think this is an odd mission because when we go out on individual missions, we take the lower grade gear. These handheld scanners and the drone are the highest caliber of equipment that we have. There must be something of real importance here.

I start scanning to the west of the west side of this building and do not have any hits. I am working in a grid pattern as my coworkers work in their grid pattern. I notice how it all seems like a choreographed dance. Everyone moves in sync in a symmetrical pattern. I keep working my area until I reach the point where another coworker has started his pattern.

From the other side of the building, I hear a coworker shout, "You have got to see this!". So, everyone moves towards her and crowd around the monitor of her handheld scanner. It looks like a little man on her screen. I have actually seen one of these before, and it may or may not be back at my abode in my treasure room. It is what the ancestors called a statue but it can be a little surprising when it first comes up on your screen because it does look like you have just found a little man. I laugh a little inside but it seems like no one else has seen one or maybe they have not retrieved such an object before. I find that the ancestors had so many different objects that the first time you come across something, it usually takes some research to figure out what it was. The new supervisor comes over to look as well. He seems quite interested in it and requests that it be retrieved. My coworker looks proud of herself for finding such an important object. Once she digs it up, the new supervisor records the coordinates and puts it in a bag carefully labeled so that all data surrounding this object is kept with this object. Many of my coworkers and all of my supervisors are highly concerned with recording all the data when we retrieve an object. So much of our history was lost during the Great War that it feels like we are rewriting the ancestors' history. The forms we fill out help also to unify the process so one agent does not record more information than another. We all record the same type of information for everything that we find. Maybe I should say what we find and turn in because some of my treasures are completely undocumented. I do not take anything to my treasure room that is important to history. Mostly they are little finds that I find interesting.

I wonder what this statue was for. The one in my treasure room says "World's best dad" and it is a male figure holding a golf club, which is another object that I had to research. The game of golf seemed to be a silly one. I think you had eighteen places to chase a little ball with a metal club and try to put it in a little hole. The description of the game was sparse but it seemed like there were many places to play this golf game so it must have been a popular silly game. Also, each of these golf places were different. There was no government regulation concerning these places. How odd.

The flying drone is done with its scan so while the supervisors are looking at the data, we take our handheld scanners and start a grid inside the building. I am positioned in the middle of the building. I see an interior wall and start scanning to the right until I see the next interior wall. I follow one of the two parallel walls until I meet a perpendicular wall and follow that until I reach the other interior wall. This is definitely a room. I start my scan from wall to wall moving from the exterior wall to the perpendicular wall that I found. There is a round object, an oval object and a large rounded rectangular object. These all appear to be made out of a solid material, the scanner is analyzing the material. Porcelain. That is not a material I have come across before. I look up and all of my coworkers are looking at their screens with a bewildered look on their face. I say, "Porcelain?" They look up at me and nod their heads. There are porcelain objects where every coworker is standing. That is interesting. Why would this building be filled with so many of these objects and in every room? I continue scanning my designated room. There is another wall but it appears that it does not span the room, there is a hole, maybe there was a door there. Okay, so the porcelain objects were in a smaller room off of the main room. Interesting. I continue my scan to see different wood structures but they are not intact so it will be hard to understand what it was. I finish scanning my defined space and move to the next area. It has the same layout. I walk over to where the supervisors are looking at the data that came from the drone. This whole building except for some rooms at one side look the same. I will have to research what porcelain was used for and what these three objects were. I remember reading about a religion where there were shrines to gods and goddesses. Maybe because there is evidence of these three objects in every room, this could have been a religious place and they worshipped the porcelain gods and goddesses. Nobody finds anything else of significance and we start to pack everything back into our transport. I ask one of the supervisors that I know has been in the department for a while what this place was and what its significance is. He mumbles that something important happened here. He says that he does not have any more information than that. Again, I feel like if we had more information on some of these trips, it would make the retrieval trip easier. Maybe it is so important that only the bosses know why we are here.

I have found that researching from work tends to excite other coworkers. We were picked for this job because we are always curious and want to learn as much as possible about everything we come across. Some of my coworkers are not as curious and try to get by with the least amount of work without getting reclassified into another career, but their time in this job will be short. My supervisors will not usually let someone put in the minimum amount of work for too long. I have seen a couple of coworkers reclassified into a different department. Maybe some people have a talent for this job but if they do not do the work that is assigned to them, they will have to find out what else they are good at.

So if there is something that I want to research without others looking over my shoulder, I do it from my abode. I can access the same research databases but at least I do not have to answer why I am looking into a topic. We can edit the databases also if we have proof of a change. Only certain groups are allowed this privilege and the archaeological retrieval agents are trusted enough to have this privilege. The others allowed to make changes are professors or upper-level government agents. Can you imagine the chaos if anyone was allowed to make changes to a database that others relied on for knowledge? You would never be able to tell if what you have read was written by a professor or the garbage collector.

RESEARCH
ASSISTANCE LOG

A few days ago, we went on the group location trip to locate the building with the porcelain objects. The next day I did additional research on porcelain and concluded that the objects were a toilet, a sink and a bathtub. The ancestors' bathrooms had all of these objects. No one from my group did any additional research. I was looking for a coworker to discuss my bathroom conclusion but none of them knew anything about the porcelain. I approached two of the supervisors that went on that trip and told them I think I knew what the porcelain objects were. One of the supervisors surprised me and asked if I would like to be on the research team for that trip. I agreed, mostly because I got the feeling like they needed some help and my coworkers were obviously not concerned with that trip. I noticed that the one new supervisor that went on this trip with us is no longer around the office. I wonder why he moved into then out of our department so quickly. Oh well, I dismiss that thought and continue on with this new research.

I join a few meetings where the building was being discussed. There were multiple theories of what it was and why we were sent there. The supervisors confirm that the mission for this trip was not disclosed to anyone in our department, which does not make sense. How could we add this so-called important location to the archives if no one knows why we went there? It feels like someone somewhere knows why we went but I guess we get to try to figure out what they already know. That is part of the problem in the government, many different departments do not like to share their information. It is super frustrating. But anyways, this research team works through the theories one by one until every previous theory has been disproven. I go back into the archives where I found the information about the bathrooms and start looking at why there would be multiple bathrooms in such a small space. One of the theories included a small living place where multiple people lived close together. That theory did not hold because we did not think they would live in such small rooms. Our abodes now are bigger than those rooms are. I find a link from this page about living spaces called apartments. Then one about hotels and motels. These were for vacations so the people would have been there short term, not a permanent living situation. Hmmmmm, this makes sense. A hotel was a tall building of these rooms and a motel was usually just two or three stories tall. Okay, now we are getting somewhere. Maybe there is a famous motel that we were looking for. I keep looking and find that a famous guy was murdered in the year 1968 at a motel. I look at where the city he was murdered in and compare it to where we were looking. Yes! I found it. I let the rest of the research team in on my discovery. They are amazed that I found it so quickly, they have been researching this without any good leads for a few days. They give me the credit for the find in the archives and I leave them to finish the write up.

The next day, one of my supervisors' bosses comes to my office to congratulate me on the research. She says there are some interesting things coming up and that she will put me on the team now that she has seen my talents. She tells me that I have a real chance of standing out above my coworkers if I continue to develop my talents as I have been. This is not a normal occurrence. Our department is separated into my coworkers and myself at the bottom, then the supervisors, then their bosses and who knows above them. We do not go communicate with the bosses and they do not come communicate with us, everything goes one step at a time. I am quite interested why this boss spoke to me.

THOSE
CALCULATIONS

The way we make these calculations just does not seem right to me. I keep thinking there has to be another way to be more accurate. I revisit the work I did trying to work backwards for the Grand Canyon. Maybe if I try another landmark, I can figure it out. I pick the Space Needle. I look at the original calculations and then compare it to the actual coordinates taken on the location trip. Ok, so if I move this number that was in this equation here instead of there it results in the actual coordinates. Wait, why did that work? Let me try another one. I look at the way the Golden Gate Bridge was calculated and compare that to the actual location. I rearrange the equation to match the way I did for the Space Needle. Yes, that worked again. Ok, maybe just one more example. I look at how the original calculations compare to the actual location. Again, rearranging the equation results in the actual location!

If this is the case, why could I not figure out the Grand Canyon location? I take this new method of rearranging the equation and once again come out a different location that what is recorded as the actual location. This is really bothering me. I decide that I have to go see the Grand Canyon with these calculations. Maybe this solution is easier to find when you are there, like the metal chair solution. There is not enough time left today so I will go tomorrow.

The next day arrives and I sign out a flying apparatus on a trip to the Grand Canyon. It takes a while to get there so I look around on the flight there. The landscape of this country is so different from one part to another. There are rivers in the section I am over now but I know that shortly there will be very little in the way of rivers, ponds and lakes. Now the section I am over is dry. It is no wonder that this section burned so easily, there is no water around for hundreds of miles. I soon land and compare my location to the actual location as stated in the original find for the Grand Canyon. I am at the exact spot. I walk around and look around. I get back into my flying apparatus and fly to where the calculated coordinates are. Ohhhh, I see now. This landmark is so large that the new calculations take you to the middle of the location but what the first retrieval agents mark as the actual location is where they landed. It makes so much more sense now. When the landmark is as large as this one, the coordinates should almost be more of a range. It would be more accurate to say it spans from these coordinates to those coordinates. But when the landmark or object is just one thing or a lot smaller than the Grand Canyon, my new calculations will work.

I wonder why it took me so long to figure that out. Oh well, the next question is I wonder if I should tell my supervisors. This is the kind of individual thought that is discouraged by the government. They really want everyone to conform to their rules and I do not think that I want to call this attention to myself. Maybe it will be better if I keep this new way of working the calculations to myself. I return late and just head to my abode for the evening. I am excited about my new calculations but cannot think of anyone to share my exciting idea with. Days like today, I end up going to sleep without eating my dinner food rations. Some days I just arrive back from a long trip and do not feel like eating. I have noticed that there are extra meals left when my next set of government meals are delivered.

INTRO TO CLIENTS LOG

I have been working in the archaeological retrieval department for a few years now and I have been very successful in my missions, both retrieval missions and research missions. Many of my coworkers have come to me with questions or when they need some assistance. I have helped advance the knowledge in the archives and many of the treasures I have been sent to find are in the museum. We are trained from an early age to be humble but we can acknowledge our accomplishments as long as it is not phrased as a comparison. I would not say that I am better than someone but I can say that I have developed my talents successfully. I lead a pretty normal life for someone according to today's standards. I work and then go home and eat, do some additional research, then get some sleep. I have quite a normal routine.

One day, I received a communication stating that this person has heard of my talents and they wanted to hire me, outside of my government job, to go on a retrieval mission for them. They would pay me well and if I accepted this job, there were other people who were looking for someone with my talents. I sent back a communication saying I had to think about it because there was a great risk on my side if I were to be caught. The government looks at things in a very black or white mentality and this was definitely a grey area. There are government advertisements stating how not to eat any food except the government food, you should not do anything outside of what you have been trained for, the government is there to control the people so things do not end in another Great War. The last Great War was so catastrophic that it took out 99.95% of the population of our country alone. And not to mention the resources, the wildlife, the structures, so many things that the ancestors had are gone.

Throughout my life and my education, the people of today have been exposed to these government advertisements. It works almost like a scare tactic. Do not do this, do not do that, only do what we tell you to do. So when I got this communication my first thought was that maybe this was a test from my supervisors to see if I could be convinced to do something illegal. I know there are different types of tests that my coworkers have to go through but I have not heard of a test like this.

I went to work the next day and casually asked around if our supervisors had tested anyone in the department. Their answers surprised me at first because they all answered yes. But they explained about the little mini tests that we all went through at the beginning of our careers to see where we would fit best. No, I meant lately. No, none of them had. Some thought maybe I was referencing the open cases we routinely work on as a test and that was not quite right either. So I felt safe in assuming that my private communication was a legitimate business offer. Although I would still have to be careful on how it proceeded. I do not want to do anything that would jeopardize my job. I weigh out the pros and the cons for this job in my mind and decide to try it. I send a communication back to this unknown person and say I will try it. They send some additional information about where they think this object is, it's dimensions and where to bring it to exchange the object for payment after the trip. They restate how important it is to not alert anyone else in my department and to not call any attention to myself. I just need to act like normal. Yeah, I think, that should be easier said than done. I look at the information and work out the coordinates I need to get to and a flight path. I also think of a way to leave work on a mission in the same direction so it will not look suspicious at all.

The next day I go through my open cases and find a small one that I have not closed because it seemed too small to deal with. I work through all of the mandatory steps and set out on this mission to retrieve the little object that is wanted by the government. After I find that object, I will continue to the other coordinates and find this new object.

Everything is simple with the first object and I was right, this mission alone is a waste of my time. I head to the second mission. I get to the place that I have calculated the coordinates and get out my metal detector. I start sweeping over the ground and within a few minutes the metal detector shows I have found an object. I dig it up and look at it for a while. I have not come across this type of item before. It is metal with two openings on the top. It has an electric cord attached and a metal handle that raises and lowers a little shelf in the two openings. This is an interesting find. I take a picture of it. My client called it a toaster and I have already done some research into it but it did not quite prepare me for holding this object in my hands. The purpose of this thing was to toast bread. I am a little confused why the client would want something like this when we receive all of our nutrition from the food pellets we get from the government. Where would he have the bread to need this toaster? So many questions. I clean off as much dirt as I can and put the toaster into my flying apparatus. I set the coordinates for the drop off location and I head towards the city.

Once I get to the location, I see a person standing in the middle of this abandoned street. He walks towards me as I land and introduces himself as the person who sent the communication. I simply ask him how he found me and he said that he had some sources with information. Okay, I understand the need for anonymity. I hand him the object and he hands me the exact payment he promised in the communication. He says that the object is not very important to him but he has come across some maps from the ancestors and he wanted to test the authenticity of the maps and test me to see if I would bring attention to this deal from my government agency. I reassure him that where I love my job, I would not do anything to call attention to him or jeopardize my job. He smiled at that and says there will be more communication from him and some of his friends who are interested in finding things outside of the city walls. I am okay with that and this extra money is nice too. Almost everything we need we get from the government but we also get paid from our jobs to pay for things that are not provided. No one will ever have an excess of money like some of the ancestors but everyone lives very comfortably. There are no poor people and there are no rich people. Everyone would be considered middle class because that is the way that the government wants it to be.

There are no crimes between people of different classes. There is no need to steal from the rich to give to the poor.

A few days pass with everything going smoothly as normal when I get another communication from a different client. I think that since the first one went so well that I will try another one. This one was located in the city of replicas. Great, I always enjoy trips there. I work out the coordinates and then set up a retrieval trip for my job that is more of an expedition where I go and see what I find. This way there is no pressure on finding anything to bring back. The communication also has coordinates for a place to meet up that is in the same abandoned part of the city where the other drop off place was. I send a communication back to this client saying I will go on this trip, the day I will go and that I will send a communication with a time that I will be returning.

I head to the city of replicas and search for another tall building that I have not seen previously. I find the building and find the entrance. Some of these buildings survived the fires because of how much water was in them, around them and they had fire protection systems. Some of these buildings are falling down and some are still standing. This one seems to be in pretty good shape. I head to the area I am instructed to go to and find what I am looking for. There is a huge safe which was popped open previously. Inside there are multiple containers and inside the containers are tons of treasures. There are jewels in this one, there are gold bars in that one, there is paper cash in this one, there are silver coins here and gold coins there. The ancestors must have held a huge wealth here. I do not know how you would spend the jewels, cash or coins in the city without bringing all kinds of attention to yourself. My client has requested the one with the jewels. I wonder if they even know what else is here. I load the one container back on to my flying apparatus. I shut the door a little so it is not so obvious in case another agent comes here. I am actually not sure what anyone in the government would do with this treasure other than put it in the museum. I decide to walk to the next building on this street and see if they have a treasure room located in approximately the same location within the building. I walk in the building while inspecting to make sure the structure of the building will hold and not fall down on my head. I go to where the other treasure room was and yes, this building has one also. The safe door is again open and there are plenty of containers with plenty of valuable items. Ok, I think I will try one more building. The next building on the street did not fair too well and is creaking as I walk up to it. No thank you, I do not feel like dying today. I will find another building. The one across the street seems like it is sturdy and there is no creaking. Once I enter the building, I again walk in the same direction as the other two treasure rooms but this building is set up differently. It takes me a few more minutes but I find the treasure room. This one easily has more than the first two buildings combined. I just cannot imagine how much this treasure would have been worth to the ancestors. Maybe I should call this the treasure city instead of the replica city. When I am coming out of this building, I think I should take my flying apparatus on a low fly through this city. This city is quite large and maybe I will be able to see things better from the air instead of walking everywhere.

I start flying in a different direction than I have previously flown. I am flying slow and probably only fifteen feet above the streets. I see a building that looks interesting because it has the name museum on it. Oh, this would be perfect! This would give us great insight into what the ancestors thought was important enough to put in a museum.

I park and walk into this building. Many objects are now dust but some objects remain. It seems that many of the objects that used to be in this museum were animals so their bones do not exist anymore. But accompanying each section are pictures drawn to match what these animals looked like when they were alive. I record my trip inside this museum documenting what can be seen and stopping long enough at the write ups so that we will be able to duplicate them again. I narrate this recording so if the images are not as clear, someone viewing my recording will know what it is they are looking at. This find makes me think that maybe all cities that are this large might have museums as well. I finish documenting and also take a picture of the outside of this building. I fly a short distance and see another museum building. This one says it is a museum of neon. This building has many metal signs. Some signs have a glass tube formed in letters while some signs there is broken glass between the metal parts. I record this museum as well. There are not any examples of a fully complete sign, they all have some type of damage. As I am documenting this museum, I again stop beside the descriptions so we can analyze all of the information later. I consider this mission very successful and I head back towards the city. I send communication to the client concerning my arrival time and head towards the exchange point. I am so excited about my museum finds today. I do not even know how much information I will be able to load into the archives with this new data.

When I arrive at the exchange spot, I see a woman walking towards me. She asks me how the trip was and if I found the object easily. I really do not know anything about this woman so I decide not to tell her about the other treasures in that room or the other treasure rooms in the other buildings. She hands me the payment that we previously discussed and said that I should make anyone coming to me for my services pay half of the fee upfront and the other half after I exchange the stuff. She tells me that there are some people looking to hire me for my services that cannot be trusted and to trust my instincts about some of them. If they seem funny to me then I should be extra careful with them. Not all people who will be contacting me will be nice people. I thank her for the warning and head to my abode. I think about her warning and decide to take her advice. By getting half of the payment before my trip it would ensure that the clients do not just steal the treasures from me and not pay me. What an awful thought. Maybe I should be a little more cautious with these clients. I never would have even thought that some people might try to steal from me or not pay me.

MUSEUM LOG

The next day I show up to work with such a huge smile on my face. Today is going to be great and I cannot wait to share my museum finds with my department. I call a group meeting, to include my supervisors, shortly after I arrive. When everyone convenes in the meeting room, I start to explain what a treasure I have just found. I talk about how, if we locate the largest cities, we need to see if any museums survived whatever catastrophe was in that area. I can see some of my coworkers getting excited at this idea of being able to find museums from the ancestors. I show my two recordings with the pictures and descriptions. There is so much information here that we can add to the archives. I suggest that we, as a department, split this up amongst all of the people in our department. I think one group should take the information from my documentation and replicate it and add it to our archives. Another team should start plotting where more of these museums could be found. Another team should fly to these points and document these museums. We will also have to decide what objects from these museums should be brought back to be added to our museum. Based on the size of these two museums that I have found, we could not possibly bring back everything from every museum we find. Now granted, there might not be as many items in some locations. The animal museum would not produce many solid objects but almost all of the drawn pictures and descriptions would easily transport back to our museum. I try to facilitate this meeting without overstepping my boundaries. I am not a supervisor and it is not my place to delegate jobs to others, so I try to gently suggest these ideas. I am glad that the ideas have taken hold and one supervisor steps up and officially organizes the teams as I have suggested. Once everyone has a new job, they disperse back to their offices to start this new project. The supervisor that organized this project pulls me aside after this meeting is over and tells me that we need to talk to one of their bosses. Of all of the bosses, this supervisor takes me to the boss that was highly impressed with my work on the motel from earlier. The supervisor says that I have an amazing find and precedes to let me explain what I found, how I found it, and how my plan for the next steps all played out in a meeting that I called and we just ended. The supervisor is very clear that even though he has agreed to organize this project, everything else was my idea. This boss keeps looking from the supervisor to me to her desk back to me back to the supervisor. She dismisses the supervisor and asks me to sit down. She starts off with some congratulations on a job well done, then she looks at me and tilts her head a little to the side. You have a talent for this work that we have only seen in one other person, she says. Most of my coworkers are like little worker bees, they are good at what they do but cannot think outside of their comfortable little realm. They do not think about where to find new items, where to look for new discoveries, and they cannot solve the problems that I have been able to solve. She is very impressed but she is cautious because the only other person with talent like mine was my mentor and she still has not been heard from. She is happy to have me on the team but she is uncertain that I will not go down the same path as my mentor.

Wait, what path is that?

She explains that my mentor did not disappear. That is the story that everyone has been told because it was safer if no one knew the truth, and only a couple of the bosses do know the truth. This boss explains that my mentor had come to her, a few weeks before she left and stated that she was starting to see people outside of the city walls. The first time my mentor was afraid but she started to speak to these people outside of the city. My boss said that my mentor was having doubts about how good our new government really was and she was starting to think that life outside the city would be better for her.

This information is so new that I keep shaking my head. I am having a hard time believing this about my mentor and I will really need to stop and think about this, to process it. I tell my boss that even though I worked closely with my mentor, she never alluded to that secret life and I just cannot see myself following in her footsteps. She asks me what my opinion of the new government is and I have to tell her all of the things I have been taught. I tell her that the new government has the best interests of the people as the priority, that we live in peace because of all of the rules and controls that are put in place. Blah, blah, blah. I lie as best as I can because in my mind, I have already started thinking that I might have already started down the path that my mentor went down. My boss says that my mentor felt comfortable enough to talk to her when she started having doubts about the government and when she would see things that she did not report. My boss wants me to feel just as comfortable to be able to talk to her if any of these thoughts start in my mind. I tell her that I will and thank her for being so open with me. She says that not everyone in the department is the same, so if I approach any other supervisors or bosses, they may find me a place in another department. Yikes! I tell her that I do not want to do anything to jeopardize my job and with that I think she is satisfied with our conversation.

DOUBTS

I go back to my office and try to process what the boss told me. My mentor did not disappear. She saw people outside of the wall. She spoke to them and she is probably living with them. Some coworkers stop by my desk and congratulate me on the find. They say they did not want to bother me because I looked deep in thought and they assumed I was thinking about the museums. I look at the list the supervisor made about who was assigned to the teams that I suggested and I looked around the office at my coworkers. It did look like I was thinking about the museum project but what I was actually thinking was about what my boss had said. These coworkers do not think about these projects like I do. Even the motel team could not come up with the solution until I joined the party and it only took me a few minutes to crack that case open. Why am I so different? Why can I not conform like they do? My coworkers do not take little treasures home and research them at home. Sure, there are some people that do solve problems well but they do not think further than each individual trip. They do not connect the trips and see the larger picture. I also think that I remember that my mentor chose me. I think she could see that I was similar to her even from the beginning. Does that mean that I will end up on the same path? She left her job and I do not want to leave my job. I do distrust this new government after seeing how the advertisements were false about what is outside of the city walls. I have started taking on extra clients and have started making money on the side that the government does not know about. My secrets are accumulating. But I do love my job. If I were to leave the city, I would not be able to go on these trips. I would not be able to add to the archives. I value all parts of my job. I try to think back about my mentor and her mannerisms. Now it has been even longer since the last time I thought about her and trying to retrieve these memories is getting harder. It seems like it was so long ago, but in reality, it really was not that long ago. I wonder why I cannot recall details about her so easily. I try to think if there were any times that she might have said something that I thought was odd. I just cannot come up with anything now just like I could not come up with anything soon after she left.

Wait. Would my coworkers come up with nothing if I were to disappear? No, they would not. They do not have a clue to the doubts in my mind. My mentor must have been keeping those thoughts inside her head for a long time before divulging some thoughts to her boss. I am more like her than I thought. We both have these thoughts. How did she start thinking about leaving? She saw people outside of the wall. Did I ever see people outside of the wall? No, I do not think so. There was that one time I thought I saw movement, where was that?

It is still early in the day. I go check out a flying apparatus and go back to the spot where I thought I saw movement. I fly low and slow through the area. I park on a hill and start walking around. I keep my bearings about me but end up walking quite a distance away from my flying apparatus. I listen for any foreign sounds but I do not hear any. I look in every direction while I am walking but I do not see anything. I am also trying to walk quietly so I do not alert anyone or anything to my presence. It is starting to get late in the afternoon, I think maybe this was a wasted trip. I should just go back to my flying apparatus and go back to my abode. It is only when I get close to returning to my apparatus that I see something tied to my seat. I look around and do not see anyone. It is a note written on paper. It says that I watched you land and I know who you are. I am watching you now and if you want to talk, please sit down and close your eyes.

Whoa! She is here! I promptly sit down and close my eyes. I hear footsteps, she says you can open your eyes. I see her and am so excited! I tell her that I have so many questions for her but I am running out of time and will need to return to the city soon. She says she knows. I ask how she is doing but I really do not have to, she looks great. She looks better than she did when she was in the city. She has a glow about her that I never noticed before. Her skin looks good, her eyes look bright. She asks me what I was looking for on this hill that I did not take any equipment. Always the mentor, I can not believe she is still trying to instruct me even now. I said that a while ago I was on a trip in this area and I thought I saw some movement. She said it was her but she wanted to see who was in the flying apparatus and when it was me, she thought I would come back if I had awakened from the government induced trance. I said that I feel like I am awakening from a trance and do not trust the government. I have so many questions that I want to ask her but at this moment it seems like they have disappeared because I can not believe that she is standing right in front of me.

She hands me some more accurate coordinates where I can find her. I tell her that I want to see her again and there are so many things I want to talk about. She says in time we will connect again. I tell her that I will work a few days in the office and then I will come find her. She puts her arms around me and tell me that it is called a hug and it is because she is so happy to see me. I hug her back; I am so happy and so confused. I head back to my abode because I have so much to think about.

When I get back to my abode, I go right into my treasure room. What an unexpected turn this day has taken. I went to work excited about my museum find, then I find out my mentor did not disappear and then I found her! How crazy is that! So now that I know she is alive, what do I ask her first? Do I let her know about my private clients or is that a secret that I need to keep even from her? Why did she look so much better? What caused her to have that glow? So many questions. I can not wait to see her again and ask her everything I can think of.

MUSEUMS LOG

The different teams have been diligently working on the museum project. Plots have been charted and plans have been set. I have been overseeing these missions to make sure that everything is perfect. We have gone to three different museums and have brought back lots of information that we did not know before. I am super excited for this next mission. We have identified a large city that we believe may have multiple museums. We are still having a hard time distinguishing which buildings in these larger cities were museums and which were not. Sometimes the building will still have the word museum either on the building or on a sign near it. But some buildings have no markings on them. We have encountered a couple of buildings that were not museums so when we started searching around, we found it to be an office building instead.

Today there is a group headed to this city south of us to see if we can find a couple museums. Our research from other museums has led us here. We are flying in one large transport but have brought a couple smaller flying apparatuses with us for a side trip. About halfway through our trip I really start looking at who has come along on this trip. I might be overseeing it but technically there is still a supervisor in charge. I know everyone in my department but there is a new guy with us in this transport. Who is that? He is too old to be an intern. I wonder if he is from another department.

As we fly over this city towards our location, it seems like this city received a great amount of damage from the bombs. There appears to be some localized fire damage around the bomb sites but it is not widespread. Also, there is some flood damage but not much. There is a surprising number of buildings that are still standing. I think I have been on a trip to this city before but not to this part of it. I try to remember when I came here and it takes me a while to remember. Sometimes it just feels like my brain is sluggish. When I finally come up with it, I remember that it is the city that had the obelisk we retrieved.

We land and start exiting the group transport. Everyone has their tasks for this mission and everyone starts unloading the equipment they will need. The first part of the trip is to find this main museum as it should hold the most information. Finding this museum was my main objective for this trip. There are some buildings still standing but the building we thought would be the museum is not. We split up and check the surrounding buildings. If our calculations are off by just a little bit, we could be a building or two away from our target. When our destination is in a city, sometimes we will land in an intersection and not know exactly which building we are looking for.

I went into one building and from the next building I hear "you have got to see this!". I think that is my coworker that found the statue on the motel trip. Everyone runs over to the building she is standing in front of. As we walk in, we are all amazed. This is the museum we were looking for and it looks like, for the most part, that it survived intact. Yesssssss! Look at all the displays......... I do not even know which display to look at first, I want to study each one but I want to see all of them. This museum was known for its history of our country and it fills in the gaps of our knowledge of our ancestor's world. I was originally going to record this museum but I delegate that task to another coworker who is not as excited about this find and I start exploring.

As a child in school, we are taught courses in the history of our country from the stand point that our government wants us to know. I have had some suspicions that they left out major eras that did not fit into the perspective that they were trying to teach us. As I have researched more of our history, I now realize that they did not lie to us, they just left out huge sections of time that I now think is important to know. As I am looking at each of these displays, I wonder how much of it we will be allowed to incorporate into our museum and how much will make it into the history classes of the children. My excitement over this find starts fading as I think that there is a very real possibility that these finds may stay hidden. The new government is not going to want to share this new information with the people. I am feeling quite disheartened but I still want to know the entire history of our country. I wonder how many other people really care to know the truth and how many are content to know the history that is fed to us by the government. I look around at the other coworkers in this building and I can see that they are going about this task like every other task. No one is as excited as I am, except the first girl to find this building. But I am afraid she is only excited because she wanted the recognition for the find, not for the contents that we found.

I continue looking around because I want to absorb all the information I can, but I find my mind keeps wandering to the fact that I wonder just how much of this will be useful to the government. I really cannot stop these thoughts and with the concession that I will still have the recording to reference, I walk outside to try to clear my head. How can the government suppress this information from the people? How can they justify not giving the people all of the information and let them decide how to process it? I reflect on just how much we are fed by our government to lead us in the direction they want us to go. Is it really working? Are the people really okay with all of this control? I think about my coworkers and sadly, I think that the people are okay with this control.

I happened to walk into another building because in my absent-minded walking, I have ended up at another building that survived intact. This building looks like an office building. My curious nature takes over and I try to figure out what this building was. I search a couple of desks and see that this was a government building of our ancestors. I read through some of the papers and see some memos in connection with the war. I grab the entire file and start looking at other files. This is amazing, this is what I was really looking for. Maybe I should save these files for a time when I can come back without any coworkers and read them more in depth. I return to the group but pay extra attention to where this government office building is so I will be able to find it again. The crew has finished documenting the museum and start packing the equipment back into the transport. I explain that we do not have enough time to search the area for more museums and I will coordinate another return trip soon.

HISTORY LOG

I think back about the history we learned in school. Before the Great War the ancestors moved towards making everything electronic and everything was saved to what they called the iCloud. This iCloud had all kinds of data that the ancestors valued. There were barely any paper records left. There were whole libraries that were digitized. Many businesses had their entire business workings over the internet and some never had any paper backup. Private businesses, small town libraries, some banks and even some larger international businesses were fully dependent on the internet. And that is just to name a few. The ancestors thought that since they were killing the planet in some ways, they would try to save the planet in other ways. So even though they were over polluting the planet with the plastics, they wanted to save the trees by not producing anymore paper. Acts of aggression were increasing all over the world. Our country was first hit with an electromagnetic pulse. Everything that was held "securely" on the internet and in the iCloud was wiped out completely. Electronics failed and everyone and all of the businesses that were dependent on these electronics immediately lost everything. It was ironic that the government, which was often looked at negatively for moving so slow to migrate everything to the electronics, was one of the few things to survive this first electromagnetic pulse.

Our country retaliated against the country they thought was responsible for the electromagnetic pulse and the Great War began. There were bombs from different countries so the effects were different. Different cities were targeted by different countries. Some countries targeted national monuments and other countries targeted dams in order to try to flood some areas. There was such widespread destruction because no one knew where or how the next assault was coming. So many countries were involved and the devastation was global. Over fifty percent of each country's population lost their lives. Our country suffered heavy damages because we were trying to fight the war in so many different countries that they all seemed to fight back against us. The war lasted for so long that some governments of the smaller countries were wiped out completely.

When the rebuilding started, our new government decided to change some things dramatically so that history would not repeat itself. That brings us back to today. While the natural environment is healing itself and going through the slow process of regrowing, all the people were rounded up and are kept within the city walls. Once the environmentalists get the rest of the country back to suitable living conditions, the government will set up approved new cities for the people to live in. That is the plan that the government has told us. There are updates from the environmental team but it seems like we are still years away from other inhabitable cities. I am starting to think that the government wants to make sure that the people are well trained before they let them run another city. And I am sure that each of the new city governments will be run like our city government is, with total control.

I decide to go back to the ancestor's government office the next day because the papers I found were quite interesting. I fly out and head straight to the location because I want to be able to spend as much time there as possible. Many of the ancestor's government agencies were slow to put their archives into the iCloud so many were still using paper records and filing them. I know that this city was targeted in the Great War but maybe some of the government buildings were not identified as such and that is how they survived. This building is very similar looking to the museum that is nearby.

Here is the first file I saw the other day. I start reading through the memos. I really cannot believe they printed these out. Sure, it says confidential on it but these seem to be some deep governmental secrets. This first file lays out in detail a scientific description of how there is an increase in solar flares. These solar flares were causing disruptions in the electronics of the day. At the beginning of the study, the solar flares were observed with special equipment and the disruptions were so small that specialized equipment was also needed to record them. In the middle of the study, the flares were increasing in size and the disruptions were increasing as well. At the end of the study, the recommendations included not saving any important information on the internet and lessening the reliance on electronics. It says that a large solar flare is developing and the disruptions it will cause will be beyond our understanding.

This file was dated to approximately six months before the Great War started. This information is quite eye opening. The government knew that the electronics were going to fail. I wonder if the government suppressed this information from the public. I think with the widespread effects the first electromagnetic pulse had on private companies in this country, I am going to assume the government did not disperse this information. How many companies could have prevented their downfall, even with as little as six months' notice?

The next file I read also deals with these solar flares. There are some memos talking about the need to start sending paper memos again instead of emails. They also talk about printing the most important files and finding a way to save them in the event of an upcoming imminent electronics disruption. I understand how this was a good idea, but I still can not believe they did not disperse this information so other companies could save themselves as well. In fact, the next few memos go into detail about keeping that information confidential and many government offices were not even going to be warned. There is a list of which agencies were selected to know and which agencies were not going to be told. There is some communication about how one high ranking officer wanted to inform the public so they could prepare as well. His communication is immediately responded to negatively, there is no reason to inform the public. The communication says we do not want to cause panic, we do not want to have to deal with the general public over this. Wow! My opinion of the ancestor's government is changing completely while reading these files. I take a quick look at the time and decide to stop for a bit to get something to eat. I brought a little bit of a snack. Aside from the food pellets we get from the government, we have these little snack bars for times when we do not have enough time for a full meal or for those who are not capable of eating a full meal.

The next few files do not seem to have anything of too much importance. It looks like back up files of things that this office did not want to lose if there was an upcoming solar flare. However, I find this file that is not too thick but it was hard to find amongst these other files. This one starts with a memo from different officers in other countries saying that some of the aggression in other countries is getting worse. The government's response to each of the officers was exactly the same. They were told to report as long as possible and to get their safe place stocked with supplies in order to survive a war that will be starting soon.

The next set of memos to these officers say that on this certain date, our planet was going to experience a solar flare that was going to disrupt all major electronics. Our country was going to tell the people they are under attack and the war will start the same day. Evacuate to their safe places now and wait until the war is over and they will be rewarded for their loyalty with a place in the new government or a place in the governments that they will be setting up in the remaining countries. This war will last until the population of the world is decreased to a manageable size and when the world's countries are devastated, the new government will step up and control the people of the world who were able to survive.

I do not even know how to process this. The ancestor's government used a natural phenomenon to start a war they were planning in order to rule the world! This changes everything. I do not even know what to believe anymore. I need some time to process all of this. But I realize that I can not just go back to work and act like I do not know this new information and I do not want to do anything that will alert any of my supervisors to realize anything with me is different. I do know that these files are very dangerous and I am glad I am the one who found them. But, I think, which of my coworkers would ever have veered off the path of a location trip to find this. I wonder if our new government even realizes that these memos survived. I can not take these memos to my abode. I have no idea what would happen to me if the government found out that I knew the truth. Do I leave them here? What if other government agencies are looking for these? Should I hide them in this office? Should I hide them in another location? I have to do something with them. Think, girl! Where is the best place for them?

I quickly look through the other files. I decide which ones are super important and which ones I can leave here. I go into a few other offices, scan the files quickly and gather a few more files. At this point I now need a container to carry them. I find a box with handles which works perfectly. I take them outside and look at the other buildings around me. I can not take them to the museum because other retrieval teams will be revisiting there. I find a partially standing building that does not look very important. I walk inside and there are children's toys everywhere. This will work. No one will look here. I stash them in a good hiding place for now and walk back outside. I think I can hear some flying apparatuses coming this way but I can not see them yet. I run to my flying apparatus and move it quickly to be parked in front of the museum. I run inside and catch my breath. They are much closer now and I walk casually outside in time to see the group land near another building. Thank goodness that I moved the files away from that other building. I walk over to my flying apparatus and one from the group approaches me. They are also dressed in government employee uniforms but I am not sure what department they work for. I have actually never seen this uniform before. The unidentified government employee asks me what department I work for and why I am out here alone. I tell him that I work for the archaeological retrieval department. We just found this museum and I came here to supplement the reports that we did not have the time to fully fill out when we were here. He takes that information and turns around and walks a short distance away and calls my information in. I look over him and see the rest of the team head in the building they parked in front of. I do not know what that building is but it must not have been the right one because they all came back out pretty quickly. They head out in different directions and enter into surrounding buildings. I find this funny because my team just did this same thing. The calculations were a little off and you end up walking into the wrong building. Well, it is good to know that they can not calculate the exact location they were looking for either.

The unidentified government employee returns to me, says that he verified that I was allowed to be at this location but it is now time for me to leave. I tell him that my team found this museum after not having the correct calculations and I offer to help them find what they are looking for, now that he has verified that I am also a government employee. His answer is very short and to the point, he says, I told you to leave. Okay, then I just have to get the rest of my equipment from inside. He says, you can come back and get it tomorrow, now you will leave. He walks me to my flying apparatus and watches me the entire time I start it up and fly away.

At first, I wonder if there is a way to fly around the corner and walk back in to watch where they go but I am a little scared and decide to go straight back to the office. When I get back to the office, one of my supervisors is there to meet me. I am glad I came straight back. He asks me to follow him and we head to one of his boss's office. I have not met this boss before. Once there, my supervisor leaves and closes the door. This boss says that he was contacted to verify my employment and he wants to know where I was, what I was doing and who authorized the solo trip. I simply explain that I went to the museum we found yesterday to see if there was anything we were not able to document in order to supplement our report. I feel like I better give the boss the same explanation that I gave the unidentified government employee, just in case there was another communication after I flew away from the museum. I tell him that I did not think I needed separate approval for a return trip because it was under the same investigation as the day before. He seems to be okay with my answers and then he instructs me to not mention to anyone that I witnessed another government team there and that as long as I was doing my job, I had nothing to worry about. He asks me if I am okay and I say that I am fine.

I leave his office and head back towards my desk. I tried to give the unidentified government employee and this boss the impression that I was a good government employee and I did not mean to do anything wrong and that I was scared that this whole situation happened. In my mind, there are so many questions. I also am scared that I might have stumbled upon something so large that the government was looking for it to suppress it. I actually feel pretty lucky that I found it first. I sit at my desk and can not seem to get my mind off of what just happened. I go back to my boss's office and say that I am a little more scared about what happened than I said I was earlier. I asked if I can go to my abode early today to calm myself down and not let my coworkers see how disturbed I am. He agrees and I leave for the day.

When I get home, I think that I am getting really good at lying. I feel like I am collecting secrets like I collect treasures.

Maybe the government cannot be trusted at all. I do not think anyone else, including my mentor knows what I know about the real start of the Great War. I think everyone who has their doubts about the government or is living outside of the way that the government wants might be able to see a part of how the government cannot be trusted. What will I do with this new information? How am I going to not let anyone, to include my coworkers, supervisors and bosses, know that I now know the truth? This is huge and I have to figure out how I am going to process this information and what I am going to do with it.

PRIVATE CLIENT LOG

Today I am working for a private client looking for something that is said to be right about here. I have to be close. The GPS coordinates that I calculated from the initial report are right here so give or take a couple feet in each direction and I should find it. Once I find the coordinates, I walk around with my trusted metal detector and wait, did I just lose a shoe? Come on girl, pay attention to what you're doing. Beep, beep, beeeeeeeep. Yes! Okay, shoe first then I'll dig at this spot.

I am looking for a safe that should have been able to survive the fire that went through this part of the country. Dig, dig, dig, bink. Yeah, there is the top. Dig around and outline the sides. Dig farther and find the bottom. It's a grey safe, 14 inches by 14 inches by 14 inches. You know, sometimes I am still amazed at what survived. This area only had some fires so I have found more here than in other places. I finish digging out the safe and hook on the straps from my personal flying apparatus. I think the ancestors had to move between locations in a personal driving apparatus. What a waste of time that must have been. I strap down this safe, adjust for the added weight and set the coordinates for my abode. I really can not imagine how long it would take if I had to use one of those ancient driving apparatus things. What did my history professor call them? Cars? Yeah, those trips probably took all day, maybe even a couple days to get from where I am at back to the Apple. Usually, I have time to search around the site for any other treasures that survived. Not today however, it really took a long time to get to this location, so it's a trip out and back today.

When I get back to my abode, I send communication to my client that I have located and retrieved the item he requested and set up a time and place to make the hand off. In the city, there are cameras almost everywhere and I use my government access to leave the city and retrieve objects. Not everyone is allowed to leave and very few people are allowed to bring objects back in. The guards and the watchmen know me. My flying apparatus always has objects attached to it so I don't even have to stop anymore and check back in. This private client contacted me discreetly and so whatever is in the safe must be valuable to him. I don't bring in any weapons or anything else that I deem threatening. Who knows, maybe what is contained in the safe are instructions on how to take over the world. Or maybe it is a bomb. When I first started retrieving objects, I would speculate about what could be the mysterious objects I was finding, retrieving and returning to the government but now, I have seen so many objects and classified things that were previously unknown that it seems more interesting to work for these private clients.

I am meeting with this client tomorrow at a little donut and coffee shop called StarDunks. I have read that there were two businesses, one was for the donuts and one was for the coffee but no one alive today really remembers which was which. I often think about what it was like back when my ancestors were alive. Those car things, coffee shops, donut shops, it all seems like a very interesting time. I feel like I am one of the few people that actually reflect to the times before the Great War. Most people now are content with the government having all the control and doing exactly what is told to them to do. They like the structure, the regiment, the conformity. I used to be like everyone else but things have started changing. I now find it stifling, depressing and sometimes I can't wait to get outside of the city just to be myself and free. It was a long day and I feel like I am more tired than usual. I do not even eat my food pellets for dinner. I just head for the sleeping place in my abode and look forward to the vivid dreams that I have just started having. When I first started having these vivid dreams, I mentioned it to some of my coworkers and no one else had any dreams. The way they looked at me, it was as if I was infected, diseased, crazy, delusional. So I stopped telling them about my dreams and now when they ask, I make it out like it was a joke. What? Me, having dreams? No, that is not true, I was making it up.

DREAM LOG 1

One of the first dreams I had was of this place, more like an environment. I was leisurely walking outside, which was weird because if we walk outside it has to be with a purpose and at an increased rate of speed. But in my dream, I had nowhere to go and no specified time to be anywhere. I was walking on what appeared to be grass and dirt. My history professor showed us illegal pictures of what it was like before the Great War. Everything in the Apple is pavement or sidewalk, there aren't any natural surfaces. There is turf where the appearance of grass is needed. Outside of the city when I am digging in the ground, sometimes I come across dirt but it's mostly ashes or rubble, certainly nothing like this dream. I could feel the sun on my face and I tilted my head to face the sun. The warmth on my face was amazing. I could smell the leaves on the trees, the flowers on the bushes and flowering plants were everywhere. I could hear water running and found a small river that had little waterfalls in it. There was a feeling I had when I was in this dream that is hard to explain but it was something like a sense of home, a feeling of belonging, a warmth in my soul. I know it makes me sound crazy and I will never tell my coworkers about it.

Something happened when I woke up from this dream. I started seeing my world differently. The trees are artificial here, I never noticed that before. They are placed in what looks like a symmetrical pattern. There are no bushes, none at all. The flowers are all fake. How did I not see that before? I never took the time to observe my surroundings because I have always lived with the rules of this regimented government. I looked at the people I walked past and there was nothing in their eyes. They were going about their routine as lifeless robots, just like I was. Now if I think back on my life, I know that I had some individuality but that was what the government used to classify me into my job. These people probably think they are also in control of their lives, but they really are not.

It was after this dream that I found myself looking for a place like the one in my dream on every retrieval outing that I went on. I have not been able to find it yet but I am still looking. It is also the reason I started taking on these private clients, going to different parts of the country rather than just the government sites.

PRIVATE CLIENT LOG

I camouflage the grey safe and take it to meet the client. I found this StarDunks place by accident one day as I was flying out of the city in a direction I had not been to before. I was looking down, observing the city streets and noticed people walking into this place without any flying apparatus parked nearby. Actually, I could not see any apparatus parked anywhere. On my way back into the city along the same route that I exited the city on, I happened to see a flying apparatus leaving a building through a large hole in the wall. I made a note of it and promised myself I would come back and investigate later. I could not change course now because the GPS coordinates were already programmed for my return trip. When I returned a few days later, there were many flying apparatuses parked in this building. I stopped someone as they were walking towards StarDunks and asked what type of place it was. They simply said the answer would present itself to me when I needed it. Well, I needed that answer now, I was curious. So I walked into the StarDunks place and looked around. People were eating and drinking food that was not the government approved food pellets. I wanted nothing to do with it, the government claims that anything that isn't the food pellets could make you sick and die. And dying was not on my plans for the day. So I left.

Fast forward to today, I use this place frequently for a public meet-up place to exchange retrieved treasures for payment. I still have not tested the food because I still don't want to die. I am early so I pick out a table and wait. My client arrives shortly after I do. We exchange pleasantries and start the business conversation. Hi, how are you, how was the trip, did you find the place. It is the same script every time. Here is the item you requested, you have paid half of my fee upfront, do you have the second half. Sometimes I think I should just write the conversation out for these clients. The client takes the safe but asks me a question about how easy was it to find. This safe was easy to find, the client had some very good information and I was able to calculate the location easily. It seems like he wants to talk more but does not, he stands there quite awkwardly for a minute. He hands me the payment and says he will contact me soon about another retrieval trip.

GROUP MISSION LOG 2

We have not been out on a group search in a while when we were called to a meeting. This group will be leaving tomorrow so everyone has to finish up their current cases as best they can. Everyone who is at the meeting will be going. I look around and see which of my coworkers were picked. I see that there will only be two supervisors going with us. The supervisor that called the meeting I know but the other supervisor is a new girl that I have not seen before. She is looking around the room just like I am. She keeps looking down at something in front of her. I wonder if it is a list of my coworkers and I.

There is nothing really exciting the rest of the day except this new supervisor is walking around and observing us while we work. When there are new people that come unannounced into our department, it always makes me question who they are. Our department is a pretty technical department so if a person can not make it in our department, they can be reclassified into another job, and there are plenty to choose from. But there are not many jobs where you can be reclassified into our department. If someone has just finished their studies, they become an intern first then they choose where in our department they will fit. So it is odd for someone to just come right into our department and go to a supervisor position. Also, another thing that usually does not sit right with me is that when we get a new intern, there is an announcement like, please welcome this person into our department. But when these new supervisors show up, there is no announcement. It is so odd.

The next day we get to work and everyone starts gathering the tools that we will need. The supervisors grab the ground penetrating laser radars. We take a group transport out to the location. This is a large area that they are calling a junkyard. There are rows and rows of automobiles parked here. We are assigned different items that we are supposed to look for from different types of cars. This is going to go into our museum in a new display about these automobiles. First, we mark the outer locations of this junkyard. Then the supervisors send the laser radar drones. Since almost everything here is going to set off the metal detectors, we are told to start heading to our locations when the drone has cleared out of our section. There is no need to check outside of our perimeter.

I take my metal detector and a shovel over to my location. I am in one of the farthest locations. My task is to find a rear-view mirror. I wonder why the ancestors called this a junkyard? Is there a house nearby and this was actually someone's yard? Who knows? I look at the location, there should be plenty of automobiles here so I am just supposed to dig on one side, open a door and get the mirror from inside. That does not seem to be too hard. You can see how the dirt has fallen over these automobiles and can make out where one is. I do not know which will be easier to dig up so I just pick a bump at the end of a line and start digging. This dirt is not too hard to move but the more I dig, the better I can start making out the dimension of the door. I get a couple of feet down and have not made it to the bottom yet. I think this task might just take all day. I dig a couple of more feet down all the while lengthening my hole because this door is kind of long.

I am only about half way through and I stop and look up at my other coworkers. I see some are having just as hard of a time that I am. The supervisors are walking around checking on everyone's progress. I start digging again. I finally reach the bottom of the door at the length of the door. I find a latch and try to open it but I did not dig my hole wide enough to get the door open. Not being familiar with how these automobile doors work, I now have to start digging my hole wider. You know, it would have been helpful if they would have showed us the best way to get the parts we were looking for. Maybe if they would have told us how these automobiles functioned, we would have been more prepared. I really feel like they have wasted so much of my time already. It is so frustrating that we do not have all the information we need. About this time, the supervisor I know makes his way over to me and asks how it is going. I mumble and grumble about how I did not know how the door worked and so I have more digging to do. He says that some of my coworkers mentioned the same thing so he will add it to his report. Then he walks away. Oh sure, add it to the report, that will help me dig this hole. Jerk.

I finally get the hole large enough to open the door and the smell that comes out is horrible. It makes me gag it is so bad. I look in and find the rear-view mirror and it has this metal beaded thing hanging off of it. When I get the mirror off the large piece of glass, I can see how to remove this beaded thing. I put that in my pocket because it is going in my treasure room. I spent just a few more minutes looking in this stinky automobile. There is a skeleton of a small animal in the back, which explains the smell. I open different little compartments and there is a gun in one compartment. Yikes! I wonder why the ancestors felt like they needed a gun in their automobile? The owner of this automobile must not have felt safe. I do not see anything else that is interesting and I think about taking the gun for my treasure room but decide to leave it here. I climb out of the car and then out of this hole with the object.

I head back to the area near our transport where the others who are finished have started gathering. Most of my coworkers had a hard time digging down far enough to get in the automobiles as well. We start comparing objects. One is called a steering wheel, which was not easy to get off. One coworker had to get the whole seat out, but it was this larger guy, so he was strong enough to get it out of the automobile. A couple people were sent after something called a hood ornament. No one had an easy task today. When everyone finished their tasks, we load everything up and head back to the office. It is later than usual so we are told that it will be noted in the report that we arrived late and it was a hard day. Okay, thanks, that really helps my sore arms from all the digging. We all head to our separate abodes. I am so tired that I do not eat my evening portion of food pellets.

DREAM LOG 2

I had this one dream that is still very clear. I was in this place with lots of foods, I think it was called a buffet. That name, buffet, came to me in my dream and after I woke up, I had to research it because the word was foreign to me. There were so many different types of food in a line, and so many different colors, different smells, different textures. It was amazing. In my dream I tasted all types of different foods and they were like nothing I have ever experienced before. The food we eat now is controlled by the government. They are produced to have a controlled number of vitamins, minerals and calories. They are small grey pellets that we add water to and put into a machine that hydrates the pellets into a mushy bland meal. I never had a problem with our meals before this dream. It provides everything we need, just like our government.

Back to the food in this dream, I can still remember how it smelled and how the smells seemed to make every bite that much better. Oh and the textures, I crunched something with my teeth. I have never done that before and the feeling from actually chewing food was incredible. I am getting this weird sensation in my stomach now as I think about it. I really want more of that food.

When I wake up, I wonder if I had this dream because I have noticed the food and the smells from StarDunks. I did not directly observe them but I noticed them in the background. I also wake up and remember that I did not eat my evening portion of pellets the night before. I wonder if the government would ever make food pellets that tasted like the food from my dream? I wonder if they would be able to make pellets that tasted like food and still have all of the nutrition that we need? When I wake up, I am also sore from all of the digging from the day before. We do not have anything to take the pain away but I feel like the more I move the better it gets. So I make my morning portion of food pellets and head to work.

STARDUNKS LOG

I have used this place for quite a number of retrieved object exchanges with my private clients and have not tried the food yet. I have noticed some repeat customers so I start wondering if the government advertisements about the food are wrong. I mean, the government ads were wrong about the violence and the beasts, or lack thereof, outside of the city walls. I wonder how many of the government advertisements are wrong. This food will not kill you if you eat it, these people are still alive and come back and eat it again. There seems to be a camaraderie between the patrons of this establishment and they seem to enjoy meeting here. There is always a loud laugh here and there.

So today I decide to visit this place without an exchange to see what the food and drink is like. I walk up to the counter and say something stupid like I have been here before but have not tried anything yet, what do you recommend. The person behind the counter sees how awkward I am and puts me at ease. We start out with a basic glazed donut and a black coffee with cream and sugar. The cashier says that this will help determine which ones I will like and which ones I should try next. He also asks if I have tried any other food outside of the food pellets. No, I have not because up until recently I thought I would die if I did. He adds a grilled cheese sandwich to the order. He says the donut will be sweet, which some people really like. The grilled cheese sandwich will be savory, which other people really like. The coffee might make me feel like I have some instant energy and the cream and sugar will make it taste better. Ok, let's just see what this food is about. I pay for my order and take my tray to a table. I know people are looking at me but I try the food while they are looking, just in case I die, someone will get help. The coffee is hot but as I sip it, there is this flavor that I can not quite describe. It is not what I was expecting but not terrible, just not great. I try a bite of the grilled cheese sandwich and I think I have been transported to flavor town. Hello, this is amazing. One more bite, oh this is the best thing, I can feel something all warm and tingling in my insides. There is no scientific way to describe what I am feeling. It reminds me of a dream I had. I eat more and more until I finish the sandwich. I try another sip of coffee. Nope, still having a hard time drinking it. I assume that when I try the coffee, I am making a weird face because someone from another table comes over to join me. She tries to get me to describe what I do not like about the coffee. I am just not sure but it does not taste good. She says she does not like the taste either but there is a flavored creamer that she uses that might help. She pours some in my coffee, stirs it and encourages me to try again. I notice that the color has changed from darker brown to a light tan. Ahhhh, now it is so much better. Actually, it tastes really good now. I ask her what she added so the next time I come here I can add it also. She said it is called hazelnut creamer. Ok, I can remember that. I ask her to stay because I feel like talking, which is weird, I usually like to be by myself and not talk to anyone. I take a small bite of the donut and feel like I am going to fall off of my chair. The grilled cheese sandwich was amazing but this is better than that. Better than amazing, I realize I said that out loud and now this girl is laughing at me. She says that everyone who comes here for the first time has similar experiences. There is something on the menu that will taste so good that you just can not help but to smile, say positive things, it really kind of expands your taste preferences from zero to infinity. I ask her how long she has been coming here and how she found out about it. A coworker told her and usually only people who have been there will tell others about it. But, she says, you can not tell anyone in the government because they are always trying to find these places and shut them down. After trying this new food, I will definitely not do anything to jeopardize it, I do not even know which department would be trying to find this place. I wonder if it would be the same department that I came across earlier when I found the mystery papers. Those employees were pretty scary. I wonder if they are the ones that are out looking for these places. Maybe they work for the truth-suppression team. That seems like a good name for them. I talk to this girl for what seems like a long time. She is so easy to talk to that when I leave, I think of her as my new friend.

PRIVATE CLIENT LOG

I am contacted by the client who I retrieved the grey safe for and he wants to meet at StarDunks to discuss the next mission because it is complicated. I readily agree because I have been waiting to go back to this amazing place. I get there a little early and try two new items, a white chocolate mocha and a spinach and egg croissant. I sit at a table and start enjoying my amazing new finds. This white chocolate mocha is so much better than the coffee with creamer. This is my new favorite, but then again, every time I try something new, it is my new favorite. The spinach and egg croissant is so flavorful. I really love this place. I see the girl who gave me the creamer and she comes over to the table. I talk with her for a few minutes but then my client arrives and I ask her politely if I can speak with him then I will visit with her again.

We discuss this new mission. It is a long trip and will require a few days to locate and identify a landmark. It is in a different country and it is across an ocean. This will take a lot of preparation because I have not flown across the ocean before and I am not sure what the process is to work in another country's area. He says that there is an area that used to be known as Egypt and he has heard of some great treasures that can be found there. He has found some war maps that show the bomb locations. With this information I should be able to locate a certain type of glass which results when bombs explode in the desert. This client wants some of this glass. I explain my ordeal of checking into the flight over there and into the cooperation with another country's government. I will send him some communication when I find out how possible the trip is. He tells me how much the payment will be and now I am super motivated to make it happen.

I think back to the papers I found saying that the officers would be rewarded for their loyalty by securing a place in the new government or in the governments of other countries. If I go to another country, will I find that it is run by people who were trained by the ancestors' government to run it like our new government?

NEW CLOTHES LOG

After he leaves, my new friend comes back over to my table. She asks me how I like the food and the coffee. I tell her that I am enjoying it immensely. We talk for a little bit but it seems like she is nervous. Then she asks if I have told anyone about this place. I reassure her that the only people I have told are my private clients. She wants to clarify that I have not told any government agent about it. I tell her that I would not tell any government agent because I would not want to jeopardize this place being taken out by the government. I even tell her that I just do not believe all of the government advertisements saying that only food pellets are good for you and you will die if you eat anything other than the pellets. Good, she says. It seems like such a weird conversation then I ask her why she is bringing it up. She takes me into the bathroom and we stand side by side in the mirror. She asks me what the difference is. It is then that I realize I am in my retrieval agent uniform that says government employee down the sleeve. She is not wearing a uniform at all. How did I not notice this before? She has on clothes that are not a part of any uniform I have ever seen. I apologize for making her and anyone else nervous by being there. I think back to all of the times I have come in here wearing my uniform that says government employee on it. What an oversight, but until now, I never noticed what anyone else was wearing. We go back to the table and I look at everyone that is in here. Everyone else is wearing these other clothes. I see all combinations of other clothes. I ask her to please pass it along to the others that I am sorry and I never even realized I was not dressed as the other people. Then I asked her where I could find some of these other clothes. She will take me there. Perfect!

We finish our coffee and leave. We walk through a couple of other buildings and come out in a covered alley. There are small shops on both sides of the alley. One shop sells clothing, one shop sells jewelry and there are more shops that I could not see into from here. I see the reason that it is in a covered alley, these are exactly the types of shops that the government shuts down. This is a place someone could express their individuality and that is not what the government wants, at all. We walk into the shop for clothes and my friend tells the employee that I have just noticed I was in uniform so we are starting from the beginning. She explains that once you start wearing these other clothes, you find your "style". Things you like, things you do not like, different materials you will like better than others. So we start with some basic pants, these are called blue jeans or denim jeans. They pick out a couple of sizes and I try them on in this tiny little room where I bang my elbows and knees into the walls. One of them is too tight and one is so big it slips off of my hips. The last pair is perfect but they feel funny because they are so different from my uniform. I have had different uniforms starting with my school uniforms, then my internship uniforms but they are mostly loose fitting and most of the uniforms are one piece of material.

Next, we look for some shirts. There are all kinds of colors, all kinds of patterns, all kinds of materials. I start to feel a little overwhelmed because I just do not know the difference. My new friend picks out three shirts for me to try. So I go back to the tiny room. I really like the first shirt and it fits well. The second shirt is a little too poofy. I like the third shirt also. So I take these back to my friend and she says the last section is socks, underwear and bras. Again, there are so many different choices. I pick some plain socks, a plain bra and some plain underwear. She takes them from me and says they are a little too ordinary. She picks out some crazy socks and some bright colored underwear and a black bra. She says that when I am feeling daring, I should wear the underwear and the bra under my uniform and I will know the difference but no one else will be able to tell. It is like having a secret all day. I pay for these purchases and the employee asks if I would like to wear my new clothes when we leave. I say that I would like to wear my new clothes and she says to take them into the tiny room and change, she will put my uniform in a bag so no one else will have to see it. My new friend asks if I want to do more shopping but I am really still overwhelmed with all the choices in the clothing store, so I tell her that maybe we could go look at the other stores but I do not want to buy anything else. We walk into the jewelry store and look at all of the beautiful jewelry. We walk into a shoe store next. There are so many choices. I apologize to my friend but I have seen enough for the day. I ask her where other people change from their uniform into these other clothes. Our abodes are too close to each other, you cannot leave your abode in these other clothes. She says there are little changing rooms in the area where we park our flying apparatuses. That is good to know. I take my new clothes into one of these little rooms by my flying apparatus and change back into my uniform.

After I return to my abode, I take my clothes inside and put them in my closet. They look kind of funny hanging next to my uniforms. I wonder if my new friend has more clothes in her closet. Maybe I will ask her the next time I see her. I am glad she showed me all these new things. I am excited about all of the possibilities of become an individual. I hope I will still be able to conceal this individuality at work though.

Two days after my new friend helped me pick out clothes, I was called for a museum duty, which I have not had in a while. I was giving a presentation about some of our newest finds and she came in as part of a group. I did not recognize her at first because it was the first time I saw her in her uniform. My first thought was yay, here is my friend. My second thought was that there is no reason I should know her and I cannot let it show that I do know her. So I went about my presentation without interruption. Keeping my secrets seems to get easier the longer I do it.

MENTOR WISDOM LOG

I have been a little busy around the office but I have been thinking about finding a reason to go see my mentor again. I have been having more doubts about the government and I actually would like to discuss them with someone and I feel like she would be the best person. Today is my birthday and even though we are discouraged from celebrating this type of individuality, I feel like I want to celebrate. I sign a flying apparatus out on an unspecified mission trip. I first stop by my abode, grab my other, non-uniform clothes and fly towards StarDunks. I park and change my clothes. When I walk in, I am already starting to feel a little less depressed. My mind starts playing a song I have heard a couple times, "I can see clearly now the rain is gone . . . It is going to be a bright, bright, bright, bright, sun shiny day". I go to the counter and say today is my birthday, what amazing drink do you recommend for this special day? Try this caramel macchiato frappaccino. The girl at the counter tells me that it is made with ice so do not drink it too fast or you will have a pain in your head called brain freeze. Okay, can I have two? I pay for them and take them to the flying apparatus. I set a course for the location where I think I can find my mentor. I get to the location and pull the two drinks out and wait. I try mine and it is really good. There is a new flavor, it must be the caramel. I wait just a few more minutes and I see my mentor approach. Interesting that I still think of her as my mentor when she has not been in that role for a while.

She says it took a minute to recognize me without a uniform on. She is wearing something that is one piece like our uniforms but the bottom half is flowing instead of being like pants. I offer her the second drink and tell her it is a caramel macchiato frappuccino. I warn her about the brain freeze. She gives me a funny look and asks me where I got this drink. I said at a place called StarDunks. She says that she knows the place well, she used to go there a lot when she first started having doubts about the government. She said that she also bought clothes from the store and asked me about a few of the people that might still be going to the StarDunks. When she describes my new friend, I say I know her. This new friend helped my mentor find the people outside of the city walls and she missed talking with her. I say that I have enough uniforms that I could dress her in one of my uniforms and I could bring her out here. My mentor's face lights up and says that is a fantastic idea! Which brings me to my first of many questions. Why does she look so much better than when I first knew her? She says it is the food. The grey food pellets also have something in them that suppresses the need for individuality. It keeps everyone peaceful and nonviolent. It works because it sedates the general public. I have not noticed a big difference yet because I have only eaten a couple meals of normal food. She said she first started noticing the difference when she would be out on a long trip and not eat the food before she went to bed. She would wake up the next day and somehow just feel better. Oh, that makes sense. There are times when I come back from a long trip and did not eat the pellets either. I wonder if that was when I started having the dreams. I ask her if she has had any dreams. She says that she does and she has them almost every night and they are wonderful. Oh good, I am not alone. I tell her that I have had a couple of dreams. She tells me that the more I can eat normal food and stay away from the pellets, my brain will respond in so many wonderful ways.

She says there are some people who have stopped eating the pellets and instead eat real food all of the time. She also warns me that if I draw any attention to myself, some red pellets will appear in my food rations. She has heard that the red pellets are more potent but anyone who has received the red pellets never ate them and they came out to the community shortly after that. There are other food places and my new friend will be able to show them to me. She is very helpful. I ask my mentor why she has not left the city if she rebels against the food and the clothes as much as she does. My mentor says that my new friend loves her job and can not think of a life without it. I feel the same. My mentor never loved her job, she was good at something that just did not interest her as much. I ask if that is why she left. She says that she started to see a world here that she did start to love and now she could not imagine ever going back to the city. Can I trust you not to take my secrets back to the government, she asks. Well of course you can trust me, I reply. Good, she says, then let me show you my new world. She first tells me to move the flying apparatus under a tree so that if someone else happens to be flying overhead, they cannot see it.

We walk for a little way in the direction that I flew here, that is how she knew when I arrived. There is a large canopy that we walk under. She calls it their camouflage because it hides the ground from anything in the sky. This is a little extra security than what they might need because she says the rest of my coworkers do not look around on flights and they certainly do not look down. Sunlight still passes through the camouflage and I am amazed when people start appearing. She tells them that I am a friend and there is no need to be afraid. Some of these people have survived the Great War out here and some have left the city. They are working together to make this community work. There are people who are raising animals for food. There are people who are planting and growing vegetables.

Everything is for the community. There is a river nearby where there are fish. I am amazed at everything I see and I have so many questions that I feel like I am inundating my mentor. Where did the fish come from? What are vegetables? Is there anything that she misses from the city? Could I bring her anything?

She answers all of my questions and then asks me one. Why did I come out here today? Oh, that is easy. It is my birthday and this is what I wanted to do today. She says that on that occasion, I should stay for the afternoon meal. I agree because I am really starting to enjoy this new food. She asks a few different people to make tonight's dinner a fish feast with rice.

In the back of my mind, I keep wondering if I should share my find of the government papers where they state they started the Great War on purpose. I think I should tell her, then I think I should not tell her. This information is so large that I do not know who would do what if they knew. I decide to keep it to myself for a little bit longer.

I see a person bring some fish over and hand them off to another person who in turn cuts the fish apart and starts cooking them over a fire. Another person brings in a container of these little things that resemble the size of our food pellets. This must be the rice that my mentor spoke of earlier. This is also prepared and cooked. Almost like a choreographed act, people start showing up and it seems like each person has their own task. In the end, everyone sits down at a couple of large tables and the food is brought around and put on a plate that is in front of everyone. My mentor stands up and introduces me to everyone and says a few words about how thankful everyone is to have found each other and to enjoy the meal. This fish is amazing. It tastes like nothing I have had so far and it practically falls apart in your mouth. The rice is good as well. Between bites I ask my mentor more questions, how did the others survive the war? How long has this community been out here? Did they have any close calls with any government agents finding them? Other than my mentor, how do new people arrive? Not everyone has access to the flying apparatuses. She answers with the ones who survived the war had found some underground caves to live in and did not emerge until they needed supplies. This community has been out here since the ones emerged from the cave and found each other and started working together. There was a couple of close calls until they put up the camouflage net. When someone new arrives, they always seem to have talents or skills that can help the community. So they are always willing to accept new people because it only makes the community better. My mentor said that she brought many of the people here when she had unrestricted access to the flying apparatuses. She stayed in the city as long as she could because she knew that people needed her to bring them out to this community. Maybe now that I know where this community is, she asks if I would feel comfortable bringing more people out here. That is a very real possibility seeing how much my distrust of the government has grown.

SECRETS

I go to work each day and try to behave as I normally would have. I have so many doubts about the true intentions of the government. I still like my job as it is everyday but sometimes, I feel conflicted that I am adding useless information or that the information that I bring back to the museum or add into the archives is being tampered with. Actually, that is a good idea. I should go check the archives to see what was left in there after I added the information from the museum that we found. I go to the section where the history of the country is, both the approved history as told by the government and the history I personally added from the museum. Just as I thought. Some of the history is there and some of it has been altered to fit the purpose of controlling the people. The part about the indigenous people that were here first was stripped down so it looks like they were here and the next generation was the founders of America and the next generation were our ancestors that were wiped out with the Great War. It makes it look like it was three generations, approximately sixty years from the indigenous people, or Native Americans, to the war. I can not believe that the hours I spent adding in all of the detail of each exhibit in that museum are literally gone. I stare at the information like it is suddenly going to appear. How can the government be so controlling? How can the others just not notice or just not care?

Maybe I should check other facts that I have personally added to the archives. I check a couple of facts that are there and now I wonder who is making the decisions on what information stays in the archives and what information is changed or deleted. I check back into the information surrounding the motel we found. I remember it was a landmark from a famous murder in 1968. The archives now say that this was where the ancestors lived and because the space was so small, the new government decided to make the abodes larger to give more space to us. The government manipulated the history to make themselves look better. Their lies are endless.

I go back to my desk disheartened. My work is gone. Whoever it was, whether it was the supervisors or their bosses, or possibly the other government agency, they have erased some of my hard work. There are times that I just do not know how to make it through my day while keeping up the appearance that I still love my job. I grab an easy open case file, see where the location is and decide to leave the office for the day. I swing by my abode, pick up my other clothes and head towards StarDunks. Maybe some real food and a coffee will help me feel better. I park my flying apparatus and change my clothes. I walk in and I see my new friend. She is always here. I wonder when she ever goes to work.

This time I order a coffee cake and a pumpkin spice latte and then pay for my items. I try to order something new and different every time I come in here because I never know what the best thing is. It seems like every thing I try is amazing but what if there is still something on the menu that is the best thing ever. When it is ready, I go sit in a booth by myself. My new friend comes over and asks if everything is okay. I say that for once, it is not. I am so confused and conflicted internally that I just can not make any sense of my life anymore. She says perfect! I just start crying and I cannot quit. After I finish eating, which is not easy to do when you are trying to quit crying, she suggests we take a walk. I tell her that I am really not in the mood for shopping. She laughs, that is not where we are going this time.

We walk into the alley where the shops are but this time, we walk past them and into another alley. We take a couple of turns and there is a bench on some real grass with real flowers growing nearby. How is this possible? We are not allowed to grow grass or flowers in the city. She tells me that there are some things that I am not aware of yet about this little area. She tells me about a friend she had that has now left the city. But her friend would always try to help everyone around her figure out their own problems, like a teacher. My new friend refers to this person as her teacher. Her teacher would always come around and make her feel so much better about herself, her job, and her little world. They would sit on this bench and have such great conversations that it made her feel like her world was not so bad. But since her teacher has left, my new friend has started feeling confused and conflicted also. She does not know why she wants to stay in the city anymore. She used to help people find their way out of the city but now she does not know how to get people out of the city. Her teacher used to transport them out of the city.

It takes me a minute to decide whether I should tell my new friend that I know who she is talking about. I tell her that I call her my mentor but she is the same person that she refers to as her teacher. I also tell her that I have been out to see her and shared a meal with her in the community. I say that I do not have the same access to the flying apparatuses that my mentor did but I can get out of the city maybe twice a week and can take one person at a time out with me. I can fill that same role that my mentor did. But I ask my new friend, if I take her out to the community, who would help others transition out of the city or introduce them to buying new clothes. She laughs. Actually, there are plenty of people who do that, if you come to StarDunks regularly, someone will take you as their project and help you to see that the government's way is not the only way to live. She picked me because I was from the same agency as my mentor, her teacher. I tell her that I was actually on my way out of the city when I stopped by StarDunks today. She looks at me for a long time and then says, I am ready. Take me out of the city today. Ok, do you need to take anything with you from your abode? She says she does, if I can wait for her at StarDunks, she will go to her abode and return ready to leave, in approximately a half an hour. And she wants to introduce me to a couple of people before she leaves.

We head back to StarDunks and she introduces me as the new carrier. I look at all of the people I am meeting so I can remember them. Once she leaves, I sit in a booth and wait for her to return. A couple of the people I have just met come over to talk to me. They have noticed that I would come in before in my uniform and speak to different people and hand packages over. I explain that I am a retrieval agent and they hired me to go find things for them. They ask me what it is really like outside of the city walls and I tell them what I have seen. There are places that were damaged by huge fires and places where you can tell bombs went off. Some places were flooded but are not anymore. They ask if it is true about the wild animals that the government advertisements warn about. I tell them that for as many times as I have been out there, I have never seen any wild animals to include the time I slept out there. I ask them how they found this place and why have they started to doubt the government. Mostly a coworker told them about it when they started to complain about the government quietly to each other. They have been coming here a couple times a week and most of them have stopped eating the government food pellets. They all said that once you stop eating the food pellets, it is like your brain wakes up from a fog. If I need other food, they can show me where to get some. They all suggest to stop eating the food pellets immediately and completely. I tell them I would like to see where this other food is but then my new friend comes back in with a bag and says she is ready. She hugs everyone there and then we leave.

I take an indirect route out of the city so the guards cannot see me. We fly in the wrong direction for a while and then I turn towards the community. We land and we start walking. My new friend is wide eyed and staring at everything. I tell her I was the same way on my first trip outside of the city walls. I hear this loud, surprised scream, look up and see my mentor. She is running towards us and hugs my new friend. They are so excited to see each other. I am glad this worked out. My friend says that she brought all of her food pellets with her in case they had animals to feed or maybe they could use them to fertilize the ground. She brought her clothes with her to have something to wear and to my amazement she brought a couple of books. She liked to read the books made of paper and because they were so rare, she just could not leave them behind. I notice that it is getting dark and I tell them that I have to return to the city but I will see them again. There are those hugs again. I guess I will have to get used to that.

OVERSEAS TRIP PREP LOG

A few more days go by and I start really thinking about my client's offer. How do I collaborate with another government's workers who would be my counterparts without causing suspicion from my supervisors or from an oversees government? I go search the archives to see if anyone under the control of the new government has been on a trip overseas. I would be amazed if anyone had because it seems like my coworkers would have been talking about it. My search results in one person who has been on a mission overseas. Of course, it would have been my mentor, you know, the only person that I cannot walk to her office and ask her any questions. How frustrating! I try to think if she ever mentioned leaving the country. I do not think she did because I would have been interested in it and asked her many questions about it. I can take a flying apparatus out and go talk to her but that is a process and I was just there a few days ago. I will do that as a last resort. Let me see what I can find out first. Of the different supervisors that I have, I decide to ask the one who I feel would answer my questions without trying to figure out what I am doing. I make up this cover story about the pyramids in the book and seeing some in that south western city and wanting to see the original. My supervisor thinks it would be a great trip, if the original is in the country. I tell her that I do not think it is because I have seen it in the other book I found that is labeled world treasures. That book said it was in a country called Egypt. She does not know if anyone in our department is allowed to go that far away. She says she will ask her bosses about it and with the details of my request, and the fact that I have solved a couple of really hard cases lately, she thinks it should be approved. When she finds out, she will let me know. Okay, now that I have started that process, I should go to the archives to do more research about the pyramids and the Sphinx. As I walk to the archives department, I remember that I am wearing the new bra and underwear and it does make me feel like I have a secret. I smile at that thought but I have to remember not to give away my secret. Who knows what would happen if anyone in this department found out that I have this secret? If they started asking me questions, would I let all of my secrets out or would I be able to continue the lies that I have been telling just to keep my secrets?

I spend the rest of the afternoon trying to find as much information as I can. I look at what the other country's archaeological retrieval agents have found near the pyramids. There is no mention of any glass treasures found in that area. I also check to see if there is anything about any glass being found at bomb locations. There has been some found and when sand is exposed to high heat, like that from a bomb, it produces a certain type of glass. Okay, so it is good to know that is true. I finish my research and go back to my department. It is time to go home so I will check with my supervisor tomorrow about the trip.

I go home and make my Monday ration of food pellets. I know my new friends have told me not to eat the pellets but I have not been back to get any of the other food yet. This food is so bland and boring compared to the new food I have tried lately. But I eat it for my meal and go into my treasure room to look at all of my treasures. Even from the beginning, I have been picking up treasures. I know my coworkers do not do this and I usually hide it from them. I take my time with each treasure and remember where I found it and why I decided to bring it home with me. Each one has a different meaning to me. This is the treasure from the time I went to the flood zone and this is the treasure that I found on the mission after my mentor disappeared. I have some jewelry that I found. If I hold some of this jewelry up, the light bounces off it in different angles. Some have different colored jewels in them. I picked up a couple of rings that I found together because I tried one on at the site and it fit. I put a ring on now and it feels weird but I like the look of it. I turn my radio on almost every time I am in my abode and that is still my favorite treasure. One day after listening to my radio, I noticed a song that came on that I have heard before. I tried to sing some of the words I remembered. Some songs even make me feel like I want to move around, I think this is called dancing. Our government prohibits this kind of random, nonsensical movement but I just like this song so much, I dance around anyways. Going to work used to make me happy and now I am finding that there are so many things that make me happy that the government says is wrong. I do not think I am being a rebel, but I really enjoy this new stuff, music, food, dancing, and maybe even hugs.

I go to work the next day and grab an open case file. Again, I leave and stop by my abode for the clothes and head to StarDunks. I first ask them if there are any carrier services needed today and they say yes. The person will be there in about forty minutes. I then ask them about the other food and they show me where to buy it. Just like with the clothes, they point out the basics first and when I find what I like they will help me decide what else I will like. Just like with the clothes, the diversity seems overwhelming at first but I have been able to go back and buy more clothes by myself, so I know it will get easier with time. I take my food to the flying apparatus and put it in my bag so when I take it into my abode later it will be disguised. The person needing a way out of the city arrives and we take off in my flying apparatus. I try to leave in a different direction again so the guards cannot see my passenger. While we are flying this person asks me a lot of questions. What is this, what is that, where are all the violent crimes that the government advertisements warn us about. I let him know what the things are and inform him that most of what the government says is a lie meant to control us. He has seen some of that but not to this extent. We land and he is so excited to be out of the city. My mentor and my new friend come welcome him; they both know him well.

I ask my mentor when she left the country and how do I go about it. She says her mission was set up from another country so she did not plan it. But if I were thinking about leaving the country, I should work with my counterparts from the other country to plan out the trip. She told me to be careful who I ask in the department because not everyone will allow me to go.

WORK LOG

I think that I have not been the model employee that I once was, and I do not want to call any attention to myself. I work through a few of my open cases. I close out the easy ones and pick a few harder cases that my coworkers have not been able to complete.

I pick a case that three other coworkers could not close out. At first it does not seem to be so hard; I wonder why they could not figure this one out. I read through the file, and look at what the others have added. I look through the calculations, the first coworker made a simple math mistake. I look over at this coworker. He normally does not make these simple mistakes. I wonder if the effects of the food pellets are causing him to lose his abilities? The second coworker also made a simple mistake. I look up and look around the office. It does seem like my coworkers are in more of a brain fog than normal. I wonder when this started happening, they all just seem more out of it than usual. I start the calculations and head out to find this object. I see that this object is supposed to be encased in a plastic container. The container should make it a little harder to find but it should not have stumped three different coworkers. I think about this on the flight out to find this object. Is there a reason why the government has started making my coworkers more foggy in the brain? Is the government threatened by us? What is the point of making them more foggy? Sometimes I can just not make any sense of what the government does. I used to be able to see the logic in what they did, but not anymore. I land with so many of these doubts still floating in my mind. I know my calculations are accurate and within a minute I find a very slight beep on my metal detector. I start digging down carefully so I don't crack the plastic container with my shovel. I find it and dig it up completely. The lid has two latches on the side and I open them easily. I have no idea what these things are. There was not any type of description. I take a picture but I am not sure how I will even start researching these things. I look for some identifying marks and find a couple. I load this container up and head back to the office. The file said to hand this object off to a specific supervisor so I take the container to him directly. I ask him what these things are and he calls them microprocessors. I ask him what they were used for but he does not know. It was requested by one of the bosses and when he asked what they were for, the boss did not know either. Ok, that is odd. I go back to my office and start researching the marks I found on these microprocessors. I read about them until the end of the day but I still cannot find a clear reason why the government would want them.

It is almost like someone took the fun out of this job. Every time I close one of these cases, I cannot help but to wonder if my work will be manipulated to try to control the people more. Instead of being happy that I worked through a problem and found the object, I feel like it is just a job now. I keep my head down more now and I really do not even think anyone has noticed.

I take this one hard case and work out the calculations. It seems like it is in a part of the country that I have not been in before. I check out a flying apparatus and head out to find this new location. There was a system of underground caves that offered secured storage facilities for different corporations. Apparently, some government agencies stored some high-level important documents there under fictitious business names at this location. The ironic part of this trip is that if any of my coworkers had been able to find these documents, they would have brought them back without even looking at them. I did not realize at first what this mission was for but once I saw that it was government documents, I started to get excited. These could be on the same level as the ones I accidentally found.

I arrive at the destination and park my flying apparatus. There is a large opening to walk through then it looks really dark inside. I grab a light and head inside. This place is huge! There is a directory and I locate the fictitious business name. I make my way through the tunnels and I shine my light into some of these other companies' sections. On my way out, I might want to stop and look a little more closely in these other sections. I find the location I am looking for and there is a gate system at the front. I have seen some other gates as I have walked in but this one is quite complicated. I look at the lock system but it does not seem like I will be able to open it without any electricity here. I think there must have been a card key reader but there must be a way to break it open. I follow the wires around; I follow the hinges and I look around until I find a weak point. I open the gate and start looking for a box marked with WWIII on it. I find it and open the lid. There were two major wars in the ancestors' time and they were known as World War I and World War II. Did they really name the Great War as World War III? I start looking through the papers. There is more evidence here about the country starting the war and blaming it on the solar flare. It is like these are the same copies of those memos. I flip through them quickly because I have actually already read them.

I start looking at the other boxes. Actually, it looks like these boxes were put in here quickly. There is no organization that I can tell. I wonder if the ancestor's government put these in here after they were given the six-month lead time on the war and the solar flare? The labels on the other boxes are just as clear as this last one. There is one labeled Area 51, one that says JFK assassination, one has alien technology and one that says 9/11. There are more boxes but these are the ones in the front. It looks like these are the government secrets that they printed out on paper knowing that the solar flare was going to take out the electronics. Why is the government just now trying to find these secrets? Maybe no other retrieval agent could work out the calculations. I wonder why that other government agency that I had an encounter with has not even come here to find this place. I start to read through some of the other secrets but I think maybe I should hide some of these boxes also in case that other team does finally find this place. I go back to some of the other businesses and find one that did not secure their stuff with an expensive gate. It looks like this business was one that supplied towels, sheets and other cloth items. At least that is what is says on these boxes. I open a box and sure enough it looks like towels. I make a hole behind the first row of boxes and start moving these government secrets boxes in there. I take the box that was my objective to find back to my flying apparatus.

I go back inside and spend a little bit of time looking through the other sections. I find one that is filled with cans of food, jars of food and boxes of food. I wonder if my mentor's community could benefit from some of this food. I wonder if it is still good. I wonder how you would tell if it is still good. I guess if you eat it and die, it was not good. Other businesses must have used this as a storage and others look like they used it for inventory. Like with the cloth business, the boxes all looked like they were in similar condition. But in this section, the boxes in the back look more deteriorated than the boxes in the front. One company's storage is full of boxes of paper cards. One storage contains heavy metal stamp plates. I know this because many of the things in these storage sections are marked well. I have probably spent enough time here and need to head back to the city. I grab a few samples of the boxed food to take back to my mentor and set the return coordinates. It will be too late to return to the office so I go back to my abode. It has been another long day, so I go to sleep without eating any dinner.

MENTOR LOG

The next day I go to work to hand off the file that was requested from the underground storage. The description for this file said to hand it off to a specific supervisor. Some of the objects we are sent to find go into the museum with the description going into the archives. And then there are these missions where it is apparent that the government really wants something that will not be shared with anyone else. I know what is in the file so I am kind of interested to see where this file goes. I take it to the supervisor and he says he will take it to the boss but not today, maybe tomorrow. He is really busy on another project right now. Perfect! I tell him that I do not have anything else that is important right now, I can take it for him. I can see he is a little hesitant so I throw a few details in there. I could tell the boss about what else I found at the site that was not important enough to put on the form. He looks like he is contemplating it. He looks for his form that was requesting this file and hands it to me. Okay, he says, take it to this boss.

I go into the bosses office looking for this boss and find that it is supposed to be handed off to the boss that admired my work on the motel trip. That is interesting. I tell her that I found this file and was instructed to hand it off to the supervisor but he was busy, so I brought it to her. She looks at me and then at the box. That is not how this process is made to work, she says and she looks at the form to see what I have brought her. Oh, you found THIS file? She gets up and closes her office door. So what is in the file, she asks me. I assume you looked at it.

I start thinking that this conversation can go a couple of different directions. I need to figure out quickly whether I tell her the truth or not. She has already approached me about the work I have done, she thinks I am on the same path as my mentor, she is a smart lady. And for the briefest of moments, I realize she does not look to be in a brain fog at all. I think that means she will realize the same about me. Okay, I think I should try to tell her the partial truth.

I start with, I read the file briefly. I can see how the solar flare would have caused some disturbances. I think the file explains how the government wanted to set themselves up to prosper in the event of a war. I try to tell the boss the facts that I read and I try not to allude to any of the assumptions that I made. The memos do not come out and say they are going to start the war, at least not in this file. I tell her that I think it was important for the ancestor's government to plan ahead like they did, and we are benefiting from that plan. Blah, blah, blah. Sometimes I impress myself with these lies. She seems quite pleased with these answers but I can not tell if she is lying to me like I am lying to her.

But sometimes I cannot quiet my inner curiosity. So I ask her who would want this file, are there people in our organization that already know this information? I notice that it was requested by a certain supervisor and it was requested by her, who else requested this file? Ah, she says, some information is only meant for those at certain levels. I was only meant to find the file. The supervisor was only meant to know who to pass it off to, and she was meant to collect the file and the rest of her task is confidential. She thanks me for finding the file but says that at this point, my job has been done and I can go back to my desk.

Okay, so I have crossed the boundaries. I go back to my desk. I start looking through other files that I have open. About an hour later I hear some commotion from my coworkers. From here I can see a security personnel go into my supervisor's office and close the door. There are some heated words and it ends with my supervisor leaving with the security personnel. My internal alarms are going off. Did he just get reclassified because I talked him into letting me take the file to the boss? Was it my boss that turned him in or was is someone higher than her? My coworkers start talking amongst themselves and I go to join the conversation. Does anyone know what happened? Why was he walked out in the middle of the day? Usually when someone is reclassified, we can all see it coming, the person just does not do any credible work. But this was one of the good supervisors. One girl says that when she was in the hallway coming back from the archives, she could hear one of the male bosses yelling from behind closed doors. She could not tell what they were saying but that it scared her. Then an office door slammed shut and she saw a female boss leaving that office crying. I ask her if the female boss that was crying was the one with short brown hair. She says it was. Everyone looks at me and I just say that I have met that female boss after the motel trip. I did not know any of the other bosses but she seemed nice when I spoke to her. Lies, lies, and more lies. We all chat for a little while longer but then go back to our desks because we do not know if anything else is going to happen today.

I guess that answers my question. I wonder if my boss got in trouble as well. I do not think she is the one who turned in the supervisor so for now I still think she is a good person. But with that supervisor being reclassified, it certainly confirms my fears about the government that I work for.

The next day another supervisor walks into that office and it looks like he tries to pick up the work where the other supervisor left off. Things are pretty tense in the office and everyone tries to keep their head down and do as much work as they can to avoid any other reclassifications. I know I do not want to do any other job and I think my coworkers feel the same way. I feel a little more anxious than I let on because I am not sure if the bosses are watching me or if my boss defended me to the yelling boss. I go about my routine as normal and just keep an eye out when I am in the hallway or in the archives department. It does not seem like anyone is watching me but I try to stay alert, just in case.

I spend two more days working diligently around the office. I think this is the most I have worked in my office without going out on a trip and I do not want to call attention to myself in case anyone is watching. The tense feeling has lessened and it looks like the new supervisor does not even know who he replaced. The office gossip has returned to normal as well. So I think it is safe to leave the city. I now have a few cases that I have finished all of the office work on. I grab an easy case and head out for the day. I go through my routine of stopping at my abode for clothes and that food that I brought back from the underground storage facility. Then I go to StarDunks and ask if there are any carrier services needed. The passenger will be here shortly. I get something to eat and a coffee. This food is so good, I wish there was a way I could have this food and coffee every day. To my surprise, my client also shows up and asks if I am ready to go overseas. I tell him that I think I am and I will work out the details shortly and get back to him soon. He asks if more money would make my trip details work themselves out quicker. Well, it surely would not hurt. So he gives me the full payment and says he will pay me the same amount when I return. Okay, this is my new priority. The passenger arrives and I tell my client I will contact him soon.

I fly this passenger out of the city and he also is very amazed at what it looks like outside of the city walls. I actually find it kind of fulfilling to shuttle these passengers to a better life. I park and again it is my mentor and my new friend that come out to welcome the new member to their community. My new friend has been friends with this guy for a while and she is happy to see him. She introduces this guy to my mentor and myself. I show the boxes of food to my mentor and ask is she knows how to tell if this food is still good. She does not but she calls to someone else. She walks over and looks at all of the items I have brought. These are all foods from the ancestors and where they were made to be consumed shortly after they were made, they are still good. Actually, she opens them up and says there are directions on how to make them on the box, she will make some now and we can all try it. But what about dying? Are they not worried about eating it and dying?

I talk with my mentor and tell her where I found this food and how much more of it there is. I tell her I can bring some more but only as much as one flying apparatus can carry. But I also tell her that I have been hired to fly overseas and I might not be back right away. She cautions me to be careful interacting with the government of an overseas country.

The food is ready and we all try it. This is tasty! The cook explains that there were some seasonings that came with it and it is pasta that is not meant to be a full meal but a side dish. Well whatever it was, I liked it. I tell them that if I can bring more out, I will stay while they prepare some of it. We do the hugging thing and I go back to the city.

OVERSEAS TRIP LOG

I go into work the next day and find a supervisor and say that I would like to request a trip overseas for an exhibition trip to see how some of the other world landmarks survived the war and if I can make some connections with other retrieval agents in other governments. There might be something that another department is doing that we are not doing and I can bring back some ideas to help us. My supervisor originally says something like what I am proposing is a trip that a supervisor or a boss should make. I agree but I think I have some good talents that I will also be able to share and that it will seem fair for me to ask for ideas when I am willing to help them with their calculations. The supervisor agrees and we walk to a boss's office. It happens to be the boss that had to verify my employment to the other unidentified government agency. The supervisor tells him about my request and he says that it is a very unusual request. Again, I agree but I tell him that with the work I have done with the motel research team and finding and putting together the museum team, that I am fully qualified to share how we do our calculations and I can only make our department better by seeing how another country uses their retrieval team. I also ask him to think about how much better our department was running after we started collaborating with other departments like the archives and the history departments. He agrees that it is a good idea but it is not up to him. He will go to his superiors and explain the request but he thinks it should probably be allowed because many of his superiors know of the work I have done in this department.

That is good to know. I wait at my desk and three hours later this boss comes to my desk and tells me to follow him to his office. Once we get there, he says that my trip has been approved and the flight plans have already been set up. Um, that was quick. I talked to the other supervisor over a week ago and have not heard back. I talk to this boss and it happens in the same day. I am glad that I asked for this trip to be close to where I need to go or if they would have set up my flight plans for the wrong country, I would have had to figure out how to get to the right place.

I look at the flight plan and ask to go home early to prepare for a long trip. It is approved and I leave. When I get home, I start studying the maps that my client let me borrow to make this trip. I start making some calculations on where the glass can be found. I also think about how I am going to phrase my conversations with this other government and how I am going to gain enough trust to be allowed to just fly around their country.

I go into my treasure room and turn on the radio, I sing and dance around because this helps calm my nerves. The last couple of weeks have been kind of stressful and I find that I really need to get away. With the file that I found about the government starting the war, to the unidentified government employee, to the supervisor being walked out by security. Dancing around my abode helps me to release the stress but it also helps me to stay clear headed. I go find some of my other food and eat some. The dancing also makes me hungry. Instead of thinking about the stress, I try to start thinking about this trip. I need to make sure that I stay focused on my two tasks, find my client's glass and to work a couple of days in this other government retrieval agency.

I go to sleep excited for this new adventure. When I wake up, I pack a small bag of uniforms and government approved snacks. I do not know if my apparatus will be searched and do not want the other government to find my secret clothes or any secret food. This is going to be quite the learning experience and I do not want any of my secrets to come out while I am in another country.

I leave the city and follow the flight path that has been outlined for me. I start flying over the ocean and can see the waves below me crashing on the shore. I keep flying until I can see nothing but ocean. I increase the speed because there is quite the distance to travel across. I look around but there does not seem to be anything around for miles. Miles and miles and miles of ocean nothingness. I check the map and I am about halfway there. I look down just in time to see a group of animals swimming underneath me. Huge animals, I have not seen these before. I take a couple pictures so I can research them later. I finally start seeing land in the distance. The trip to this country will take me over some other countries so I start referencing the map to see where exactly I am flying.

I am now over land and see different herds of migrating animals, I have to take pictures of these magnificent animals, I wonder what they are. There are groups of teepee tent looking temporary abodes out here. I see people down there; I mark the coordinates like I did with the migrating animals. Maybe I will try to stop on my way back to my country. I see rivers and trees and more wildlife. I do not think this area was as affected by the Great War as our country was. I see more groups of temporary housing and more people. I start to fly into the city and make my way to the retrieval department. I park and walk into the building. I have a contact person and I ask security how to find this person. He says he will take me directly to this person. We walk through a couple different sections and I look around observing everything that is possible. He introduces me to my contact and I say that I am super excited but it was a long trip. He wants to show me around his office and introduce me to the rest of the team. About halfway through the introductions I start feeling really tired. I ask him if he can show me where I will be able to rest. He gives me some directions to a vacant abode and I apologize for being so tired. He says that we have some busy days ahead of us so it is okay. He hands me a badge so that I can walk into the department tomorrow without needing to be escorted from the security guard. I leave and head to the vacant abode. I take my bag inside and decide that I am too tired to even eat. I find the bed and fall asleep almost immediately.

I have another dream but when I wake up, I can only remember parts of the dream. There are many people surrounding me with different types of clothes, some are bright colored and they flow like they are in a breeze. When I wake up it seems like it was a good dream and I really wish I could remember more of it. I get ready for the day and have one of the snacks that I packed. I look around this vacant abode and find that it is actually not vacant. There are some uniforms in the closet but also some non-uniform clothes in there as well. There is some food that is not government pellets. That is interesting. I wonder if this is a test. I decide not to take anything until I can ask my contact what the rules are for this government. I notice what is around me on the way into the department. I look at the buildings, I look at the streets, there are some things that are similar to the city I live in. I notice that there are a good amount of people who are not wearing any type of discernible uniform on the streets. That is interesting. When I get to the building, I use my badge and walk into the retrieval department. I say hello to a couple of people but explain that I cannot remember who everyone was from the day before.

I find my contact and he hands me a coffee. I look at it and it is plain black and it is in a smaller cup. It looks a little thicker than what I have tried before. I try it and it is very strong but good. When I finish the cup, I feel like I have more energy than I have ever had in my entire life! Wow that stuff is good. We start discussing what is on the agenda for my time in this country. First, they want to show me how they do things currently and then they want to see how I can improve upon what they do. I think that sounds like a good agenda. He shows me over to his desk and he shows me the type of information they normally receive from their supervisors. This has so much more information than we ever get. It shows the reason the government wants the object retrieved and how it will benefit the people. This is included in the description. He works out the coordinates and says we can head out to this location. We take one of their larger flying apparatuses and while he flys to the location I look around at all of the sites. The clothes on the people below us are bright, like from my dream.

We arrive at the location and the ground is comprised of fine sand. This sand piles up in what is called sand dunes. I have not seen this before and I actually think it looks interesting. They have a unique problem in this area where the wind blows the sand over their sites and can bury them as fast as you dig them. The sand also transforms the landscape so drastically that they rely heavily on the GPS coordinates. Basically, they have the same equipment we do. We each grab a metal detector and start sweeping the area. I head in one direction and he heads in another. We get quite a distance away from where we landed and I hear him yell at me. I head towards him, but exchange my metal detector for the shovels when I pass the flying apparatus. We start digging and hit a large metal box. We dig it out together and he does not even open it before starting to drag it towards the apparatus. I ask him what is inside and he responds that it is not his duty to look. He is sent to find and retrieve the object only. There are others in the department who will open and determine what to do with what is in the box. Well that is definitely a different way to go about the process. I ask him if they have ever found something that they were not looking for. He says like this box, he was told to retrieve the box and the contents will benefit the people. But if there is more or less in the box than expected, someone else will have that to deal with. I say that we have a form to fill out at the location for details that we may forget when we return to the office. Do they have anything like that? No, they do not and that seems like something that maybe we can collaborate on later in my trip. We head back to the office. He delivers the box to another department and closes the case on his end.

I ask if we can take a tour of all the other departments since we have some time left in the day. They also have a history department and an archival department. But they do have a couple of departments that we do not have. The one we handed the box off to is the supplemental department and they add the info into the archives to incorporate the reason the government added to the original information about why the object was needed and how it will benefit the people. I ask my contact how he feels about being a retrieval agent. He enjoys it but it seems like his job is repetitive. He does calculations and he goes on trips and brings back objects. He feels like he is a part of the bigger picture but sometimes it is hard to see how his work is important. I wonder why I do not feel that way with my job. I wonder if it has to do with the fact that in my department, we add to the archives ourselves and look at and analyze the objects we retrieve.

We return to his office and I ask him about the abode I am staying in. Why are there non-uniform clothes and real food in there? He says that it is what all the abodes have in them. When you are not working you are allowed to wear whatever clothes you like. He can show me places to buy some clothes here if I am interested. I absolutely am interested in normal clothes. But what about the food? He does not know what food pellets are. All the food in this country is made, prepared and served by people who want you to enjoy their food. So you guys do not have any food pellets? He says no, I have not ever seen any food pellets. He is just amazed as I am that the food is completely different in our countries. He says that he will take me to dinner and show me their food. That sounds great because I am so hungry right now. He tells me to go to the abode, change from my uniform to the clothes in the abode and meet him back here in the parking lot.

I head to the abode and start trying on the clothes that were in the closet. I spin around and move my arms and the clothes are just like in my dream. They are so soft and the bright colors are amazing. I even find a pair of shoes in the closet that are interesting. They have the bottom hard part so that you do not walk on your bare feet. But across the top are just straps that go across my foot and they feel a little awkward at first because I have only ever worn my work shoes. I head back to the parking lot and meet back up with my contact. He adjusts my clothes a little and tells me that I have not put it on quite right. Oh yeah, it feels way better now. I still love these clothes more than my other clothes. We go to a restaurant and he starts to describe the dishes to me but I tell him that I just started eating real food and I do not know what anything he just mentioned is. The only things I recognize are fish and rice. Okay, he says, I will order something simple for you and we can experiment with each meal, if I am okay with that. Yes, I am. I am loving all the new food that I have had so far and I am excited to try the new food here. After he orders and while we wait for the food, I explain how the government has controlled all of the food and delivers everyone their portion of food. It is rationed into each day, so you eat your Monday rations on Monday and it is like that all week. We get some snacks to eat at work but for the most part all the food is in the form of pellets and it provides everything the government says that we need. It has all the vitamins and minerals. But after I have started tasting real food, I realized just how bland and boring the food pellets are. Before I had tried any other food, I thought the pellets were fine.

Our dinner arrives and he says that he will allow me to taste his dish as well. He explains that the outside is a pita bread and inside is a meat with some vegetables. There is a sauce on it that is not from this country but they share foods between countries. I take a bite and it is like a burst of flavor in my mouth. I can not even decide which flavor I like best so I try just the bread. Um, that is amazing. I could eat that for every meal. I try the meat and think that is equally amazing. But that sauce, though. That is the best thing so far. I have a drink in front of me that he says is apple juice. So far, I have only drunk water and coffee. Apple juice is very good. He gives me a bite of the chicken that he is eating and that is good. Then he gives me a bite of this tan creamy food that is made out of beans and that is delicious as well. Everything is amazing and I am enjoying this meal immensely.

After the meal he says that his favorite band is playing just around the corner. Would I like to go with him? Sure but what is a band? He explains that a band is a group of people that play music together. Do we not have music where I live? I tell him that the government does not allow us to listen to music. I happen to have come across a radio and found a satellite that still plays music but I think it is breaking the rules by me listening to it. He says that it is encouraged here and we head to listen to this band. I can hear the music as we get closer and I like the sound of it. We go inside and there are people dancing everywhere, their clothes are flowing around them because they are dancing. DANCING! And they are doing it in public! My contact takes my hand and tells me he will show me how to dance. We move our arms; we move our legs and pretty soon I am having the best time of my life. The way the clothes feel, the sound of the music. This country is amazing. After one day I am convinced that I do not want to go home. We stay and dance for what seems like a long time but then the band stops playing for the night and everyone starts to leave. We leave and I just can not stop smiling. My contact takes me back to my flying apparatus and I head to my vacant abode. I am so tired that I fall asleep shortly after laying down.

I wake up the next day and look forward to going to work. I have not been this excited for work in a while and it feels good. I dress in my uniform and head in for the day. My contact greets me again with the strong coffee and we start our day. He has another case and when he starts the calculations, I ask if he will explain how he is doing it because it seemed like we were a little off yesterday. He starts working through them and when he finishes, I ask if I can show him a couple of improvements. He allows me. I say that his way is closer to the way I was shown at first, but I have found a more accurate way and showed him my calculations. I have been using my new way for at least two years now and it will help narrow the area down which will be helpful to them because of how much harder the sand makes their trips. We rework the calculations and take off to find and retrieve this object. My contact is amazed at how quickly we find what we are looking for. This new way will save them so much time on each of their trips. We bring the object back to the office and hand it off again. He brings me to his supervisor and shows her my new way of making the calculations more accurate. The supervisor immediately calls a meeting for all of the retrieval agents in the office and asks me to show them. I first explain that the way they are doing things works and that is how I was taught as well. But I started looking at where the object ended up being and worked the calculations backwards in order to come up with a better way. I also let them know that I have been using this new way on many trips and every time it is successful. I ask if anyone has an example and someone brings back a case that no one has been able to solve. I first show them the usual way of calculations but show them how it can result in three different locations. I go back and use my new method and come up with an exact location. People are looking at me like they do not believe me. I ask if someone wants to take these calculations and go retrieve the object. One guy says that he will go. Everyone goes back to their desk and will work on their own cases until he returns.

My contact asks if I am hungry and we go to a little cafe in this building where lunch is provided for any employee in this building, for free. Again, I am so amazed at how different it is here than in my country. We eat what my contact calls pita chips and hummus. Of course, it is delicious.

When we get back to the office, the volunteer has already returned. He said it was unbelievable how close the coordinates were to the object. He did not have to look far at all. The other department was also amazed because they have been waiting on the object for a long time to be retrieved. Everyone is excited and ask what else I have to share with them. I tell them there are a couple more ideas that I have on what we do in my department that you do not do here, but I will try it with my contact and if he approves, we will bring it to the group.

It is the end of the workday and my contact says that each day I am here we will go to our abodes, change clothes and meet back in the parking lot, like we did last night and he will show me around. Great! When I get back to the abode, I look in the closet and find another outfit. This time I put it on correctly. I put the same weird shoes on and head back out to meet my contact.

Tonight, he says, we are going to a restaurant where there is live entertainment. I do not know what that is, so I am excited to see it. Oh yeah and the food. I cannot wait for the food. We go to a different restaurant than last night. I wonder how many restaurants there are here. My contact orders for me and while we are waiting for our food, music starts playing and a lady comes out from the back. She is showing the skin in the middle of her body and when she dances, it sounds like she is ringing. She also has something on her fingers and she makes sounds when she pinches her fingers together. I keep watching her as she gets closer and my contact explains that in the history of their country, there were these entertainers called belly dancers. She has cymbals on her fingers and she dances to different music every time. Her job is to be a belly dancer. He thought he would explain this to me because he did not think we would have anything like this in my country. She does not work for the government and she does not have to hide her passion from the government. In this country, people are encouraged to do what they enjoy. She finishes her dance and the food is brought out to all the people at every table all at once. They do not want to interrupt the dancer by bringing the food out during her dance.

Again, all of the food is delicious and amazing. I try some of my contact's food as well. With all of this new food, I do not think I have tried anything that I do not like. How will I ever go back to eating the government food pellets after this? We go back to the parking lot and I return to my vacant abode. I have a couple of more days here and I still have to find some time to retrieve the glass from the location my private client has partially paid me for.

That night I dream of walking in the desert in bare feet and feeling the sand between my toes. It is not burning hot at this time of the year but in my dream somehow, I know that I cannot walk in the desert at any other time without burning my feet. There is nothing around me but I keep walking. I climb up this large sand dune and see an area in front of me that has green grass, a clear blue pond, tall trees and people around in the bright colored clothing. Everyone is so nice in this place but as I walk up to this place, I turn around and look back out into the desert. It is then that I see my coworkers in my department but they have all turned grey and move like robots. Their movements are stiff and awkward and some just fall over. I turn back around and everyone with the bright colored clothing is dancing and laughing and smiling. In my dream I realize that I make the decision to turn to the bright colored clothing people and turn away from the grey desert coworkers.

I wake up and remember every moment of this dream. I feel like it is important and that I think it relates to how much more I like it in this country than in my own country. There is also this feeling that I have a hard time explaining but it feels like I am more awake than I have been. I think back to what my friends at StarDunks have told me about how the government food pellets keep you in a brain fog. I have not had any food pellets in a couple of days and I can feel the difference. I also start to think that this must be how my mentor felt before she left the city to live in her community. If I go back to my country in a couple of days, how will I ever return to what my life used to be like? How will I go back to the horrible food pellets? How will I go back to not listening to music? There are definitely not any live bands and no group dancing in my country. These are some dangerous thoughts and I do not know how I would hide any of my secrets if I return to my office. But would my coworkers even notice the difference in me? No one noticed the change in my mentor. Plus, everyone is in that state of brain fog from the food pellets. I can not do it. I can not go back. What am I going to do?

With all of these thoughts in my head, I put on my uniform and head to the office. When I arrive, my contact looks at me and asks me if something is wrong. I tell him that I do not think I want to go back to my country in a couple of days. He agrees saying that from what I have told him, he would not want to go back either. I tell him that I do not think it would be easy to leave again once I get back. He says that he will think about it and before I leave, we will find a way. His supervisors are already impressed with the calculations I introduced to the department. He will ask if there is a way to offer me a job in the department. But for now, we have another hard case that they would like us to solve. While he works out the new calculations, I start jotting down some of the things on the form that we fill out while on the retrieval trip to add to the archives. I try to remember every section and every part of every section and find that I can actually remember all the details. I look back through this form and surprise myself at the clarity of my details. I am feeling like all of the brain fog is gone. Whatever is in the food pellets, it must keep everyone in the brain fog state. I wonder if that is why the government has us eating the food pellets all of the time so that the brain fog never wears off. Yikes!

I make a copy of this form and check that my contact has finished the calculations. We head out to the retrieval site and I start filling out the form. I add all the details that I am used to filling out. My contact, using the metal detector has already found the item so I grab the shovels. He is saying he just still cannot believe how much quicker finding the object is with the new calculations. After we dig up the item, I record more details about how deep it was, what type of soil was found around it, if there was any damage to the item when it was found, and if there was any accidental damage caused from retrieving the object. This object was a gold cylinder amulet from the ancestors of the ancestor's time. It was not housed in any container. So, as I was filling out more details about the object itself, my contact comes over and looks at the form. I am now finished filling it out so I tell him that it really does not take that much time to fill out and it will give anyone who was not here, more details in case they are researching this. I also note the exact GPS coordinates for where it was found. We return to the office and when he hands the item off to the supplemental department, I ask him to stay with me as I explain the form. I ask the person to show me who takes the form who will be inputting the information into the archives. They point us towards a girl at her desk. They take the object over and I take my form to her. I explain that in my country, the retrieval agent is the one that inputs the information into the archives but we use this form to help us remember all of the details, in case we were to forget by the time we get back to the office. She looks at the object then starts reading my form. Wow, yes, this would be really helpful when we get in a new object. Actually, now that I see this form, I see all kinds of info that we did not even realize we were missing. She says that her supervisor would love to see this and she takes us to go see him. She explains how when this object was brought to her, we came along with this form. She lets me explain what I just told her to him so that no pertinent information is lost. She tells him that there are details on this form that would really expand the knowledge in the archives. He looks from the paper to me and it looks like he is questioning who I am and why my contact and I are even in his department. He asks us to wait outside and soon a supervisor from the retrieval department shows up. And it just happens to be the one who I impressed with my calculations. She walks into this supervisor's office and a few minutes later she opens the door and invites us back in. This supervisor apologizes and says he did not know who I was and I obviously do not look like I belong in this country to start with so he did want to check what my intentions are. I simply say that in my country, I am one of the top retrieval agents in my government, I found a book with some world landmarks and I wanted to see them and see how other governments ran their retrieval departments. It is like a collaboration between countries. My contact's supervisor says that if this form will help his department, she will speak to her bosses and get her department to start filling it out. The more information we have, the better our understanding of our history will be. He agrees to support her and thinks that the form is actually a very good thing for his department to have. He does not want to cause too much extra work for the retrieval department. My contact says that other than learning how to fill out the form, it took me less than ten minutes to fill it out while on location. Both supervisors thank us for bringing this new task to their attention and we leave.

Before we go to dinner that night, I ask my contact if there is a place to buy more clothes. I have worn the outfits that were in the closet and I would actually like some clothes of my own. He looks at me for a minute and I can tell he is really thinking about something. We go to a store and I pick out some materials that are so pretty and feel so good on my skin. I love everything about this country. We go to pay for them and when we get there, he pays for my clothes. I tell him he does not have to because I brought my own money. As we walk out, he explains that my money is not like their money. I look a bit confused and he shows me his money. He is right, my money does not look like that at all. How have I not noticed this before? I think back to StarDunks, you order, then pay, then take your food to the table. Here we sat at a table, then ordered, then got our food. I did not pay for the food. I did not notice him paying for the food. What did I miss? I ask him about it and he explains that because everyone needs to eat, his government allows you to eat at any of these restaurants and that is how they provide for the people of the city. The people at the restaurant get paid by the government just like we do but their job is to serve food or to make food. A little like how my government provides the food pellets and I do not pay for that; his government provides him with food also. But here they get a choice of restaurants and a choice of food. I have no choice in my city. He says that there is a place he thinks will know what to do with my money and tomorrow we can go during the work hours. This place is not open after work. It is called a bank. Again, I have no idea what that is and so he explains it to me on the way to dinner. He wants to take me to a different place because he wants me to try all the things he loves about his city.

That brings up an interesting topic. I ask him if people ever leave this city. I did not notice a city wall with guards when I flew in. He responds with of course they do. Wait, what? People in this city are encouraged to take trips to other cities in order to see how other people live and work. That is why it was so easy for me to come here. It was his government that made the flight plans so quickly. They have not had a visitor from my country. Actually, he checked around before I arrived and only one other country has had a visitor from my government. It seems like no one ever gets out of my country. He asked me how I was able to get the opportunity to visit. Now that I think about it, I do not know how I was approved. I wonder if it was my mentor's boss that made it possible for me to come here. I ask him where the other person from my country visited. He said there is a country north of his country that, when asked, confirmed that a government employee from my country visited their government. He did not ask why or how or any other details about that trip. That must have been my mentor and I wonder what she was doing and which country it was. That thought is interrupted by our dinner being set down in front of us.

This food is from another country and he tells me to try these green wrapped cylinders first. He cuts one open and there is food stuffed inside this green wrapping. He calls it stuffed grape leaves. This is my new favorite food! He laughs. He says I say that every time I try new food. Yeah, I do say that. I laugh too. I really do love everything about this country. Tomorrow is my last full day before I leave to go home. I want to go to the bank to exchange my money so I can pay my contact back for the clothes he bought me and I still need to find time to find the glass that my client has paid me for. I also keep thinking about when I go back to my country, what do I need to do to come back and live in this country.

When I get back to my vacant abode, I look again at the calculations for my client. The coordinates are relatively close to where I am now and I think I will have to go sometime tomorrow, possibly after the trip to the bank.

That night I have another vivid dream. When I wake up, I feel really good. I make the connection that the longer I am eating real food and not the government pellets, my brain is functioning better. I remember things easier. I really can tell the difference and understand how the government keeps the people controlled with the brain fog. My plan to leave my country is coming together in my mind so much easier than before.

I think back to all the times I thought my mind was not clear. I know the longer I ate the food pellets, the foggier my brain was. How much better could I have been thinking all along if my brain power was not diminished by those stupid food pellets! That thought actually makes me a little mad but I remind myself that I still have to hide any of these thoughts from my coworkers and supervisors when I return to my country. I can not let them know just how frustrating that government is. Or how manipulative the government can be and there is no benefit to the people. It seems like all the faith I had in the government and how I thought they wanted us to be peaceful and thrive is just wrong.

I dress in my uniform and head into work. I even remember to grab my money and my calculations for my client's glass. When I get to work, my contact hands me a coffee. I really like this office. If I lived here, I know I would find joy in my work again, just like when I first started at the retrieval department. We head to the bank early and when we walk in, he tells a person that we want to exchange money. This is new to me but not for him. He says anytime you go to another country, you have to trade your money in for their money. If my trip was longer, he could take me to another country but we have no time left. After we exchange the money, I ask him how much I owe him for the clothes and he shows me using my money. He explains the difference in the money. He is a lot like my mentor. He explains things to me easily. I like learning new things and I like learning from him as much as I liked learning from my mentor.

On the way back to work I ask him if we could stop somewhere and talk. I just do not want to talk in the office. He says there is this park we can go to and he thinks I will really like this place. It is his favorite place in the city. He lands the flying apparatus and we walk into this park. There is real grass, there is real dirt, not ash, not flood dirt and not sand from the sand dunes. I can smell the leaves on the trees and there are flowers on the bushes. I stop for a minute and can hear water running. I walk over and see little waterfalls in this river. This is it! This is the place from one of my first dreams that I kept looking for on my trips around the country. In my dream I had this sense of being home and now I have found it. I found it! I am just staring at this river and the thoughts in my head are racing so fast. This confirms that I have to come back and live here. I have to.

I finally turn around and my contact is smiling. I told you this place is amazing, he says. So, what do you want to talk about? First, I tell him that I would like to take a side trip. Maybe I should not tell him about my private client but I decide to tell him anyways. I need to retrieve some desert glass that I am being paid to find. He is actually excited about it. Oh yes, we have so much of this glass, feel free to take some to your client.

Wait, I have been nervous about telling you because for as amazing as this place is, I did not want you to think that I was stealing some of your resources. No, no, he says. There are some artisans who create some beautiful pieces of jewelry with this glass and if someone wants some and is going to pay me for it, then I should go get some to take to my client. He will go with me to help me pick out the best pieces. He makes things too easy sometimes.

Okay, I say, one more thing. Over the past couple of days, I have really thought about my options and decided that I just can not live under the rule of my government anymore. I know that I mentioned it once but can he help me figure out a way to come back and live here?

Absolutely, he says. I have helped his department greatly and they have already asked him if he could find a way to ask me to come work for them. Both of the supervisors we spoke to yesterday brought up the fact that even though they have collaborated with different government agencies, no one has transformed their departments as quickly as I have. They are willing to help you as much as you need.

This is just so unbelievable! This place is so amazing. We work through the details and then we head towards the location of my client's glass. We land and find a few chunks of this glass. He asks if I know why my client wants this type of glass. I actually do not know. He says that these pieces are of average color and they will make good jewelry. It is not the best but it is from the location that my client has informed me of.

That reminds me of all the treasure I found in the replica city. I ask my contact what people would do with lots of jewels. He says that you could sell the jewels and make money for yourself but then also the jewelers would make money. In his country when people do well and have money, they spend money and so on and everyone does better. Ah ha. More details are starting to come together for my exit plan. I pack up this treasure and ask if we can stop by my vacant abode and put it in there before we head back to work. He looks at his watch and says that we have time but it will have to be quick, we have been away from work for a while and we need to get back soon.

By the time we reach the office, there is about two hours left in the work day. When we walk in the security guard is not there. The front departments that we walk through are vacant also. When we get to the retrieval department, we walk in and everyone yells "surprise!" Aaaaahhhhhhhh, what is a surprise????????? My contact explains that everyone knows that I leave to go back to my country tomorrow morning and so they threw me a party. There are different drinks and there are different desserts. Everyone is here to celebrate. He hands me a drink that he calls a cold tea and what he calls a cupcake. I try these new things and my face lights up. He says I bet this is your new favorite thing and we laugh. People around the party come up to me and thank me for showing them the new calculations. Some people I have not met before come up to me and say they are excited to start using the new form. The two supervisors that we met with yesterday come up to me at the same time and say that they hope that I agree to come work for them. I let them know that I am excited to have the opportunity and I just need to work out some of the details once I get back to my country. They tell me to contact them if I need any help and the bosses are willing to help also.

When the party is over, every one gives me the hugs. I am glad my mentor introduced me to hugging. It is quite enjoyable. I return to my vacant abode and start to pack everything back up into my little bag. I have worked out some more of the details for my exit plan and I really feel like I know what I have to do when I get back to my country and even a few things that I have not told anyone else about.

I sleep really well and have another dream. This one is half in grey and half in bright colors. I know this represents how my life is now split between these two different countries. I again wake up feeling great. Another thing I have to do when I get home is visit the food store by StarDunks so that I do not ever have to eat anymore of the government pellets.

I grab my bag, head to my flying apparatus and leave to fly back to my country. I am not looking forward to this trip but I use the time to reassure myself that I am doing the right thing. I have to keep my secrets for just a little longer. I have to finish out my exit plan so that I can live my life the way that I want to. The trip is long and I have a lot of time to go through my plan over and over.

BACK TO WORK LOG

When I return to my country, I am tired because it is a long trip. I fly straight to my abode and go right to sleep. I wake up the next day and send communication to my client that I have returned and give him a time to meet me for the exchange. I get ready to go to work and try to act like I have brain fog. I have prepared a few things to tell my supervisors.

I am surprised that one of my coworkers approaches me as soon as I arrive. She is the one that was excited when she found the statue. I have not had many conversations with her but she is now acting like she missed me. She says that she went out on a solo retrieval trip and was so excited for the object that she found. She tells me about the trip out and the dig and the trip back, with lots of details. She seems to be talking a lot, which is not common for my coworkers. Most of the conversations we have with each other are short and to the point. I am interested in why this girl is talking so much. I get to my desk and say that she seems really excited. Is there a reason why she is talking so much? She says that she has been studying some of my work and she thought I had left and she is so excited that I have returned. I tell her I was on a planned trip. Didn't someone tell her that I would be back in a few days? I ask her why she was studying my work? She said that she realized that I was the one in the office that everyone went to when they needed help, and she wanted to be that one. She wanted to help everyone with the problems they could not solve themselves. Did studying my work help her at all? She says no, she could not figure out how I knew how to help everyone else. I tell her I can teach her some of my problem-solving skills if she would like. She gets really excited about this and goes back to her desk. How odd. Did I just not notice that she was so excitable?

I go to the supervisor that helped me get the trip approved and it actually feels easy to pretend I am in a brain fog because I am still tired from the trip. I did not realize how tired I was until I was trying to keep up in the conversation with the excitable girl. I see the supervisor and ask if she has some time so I can tell her about my trip. She does. I tell her how important it is that we collaborate with other government retrieval departments like I did on this trip. I see how their departments are organized differently than ours and I describe how there is a separate department to add to the archives and the retrieval agents just go and retrieve the objects. Then they bring back the object and hand it off to another department. She asks if I thought that worked better than the way we do it. I explain that my contact was not able to see the full picture about the objects that he found. It seemed to me that because we make the calculations, we find the object, we fill out the form and then we update the archives about the item, we have more of a vested interest in our objects. I like the way we perform the tasks but it could also be that it is what I am used to it as well. I told her that it was not my decision to make but I just wanted to let them know in case they wanted to change things around. I tell her that I am still really tired from the trip and even though I just got to work, ask if it would be okay if I went back home to rest. She says that is fine. I go back to my desk and find the excitable girl. I tell her that my trip has made me tired and I will talk to her tomorrow. I go home and immediately fall back asleep. I did not seem nearly as tired when I arrived in Egypt but now that I am back, I am so tired.

I have two great dreams while I am sleeping. When I wake up, I realize that was the first time that I had two dreams in one night. I sleep all afternoon and all night. When I finally wake up, I am so hungry. I know I have some real food left in my abode and I make some. I eat it but I am still hungry. I put my uniform on and grab my clothes. What a ridiculous extra step that I have to put on my uniform and then change into my other clothes. I cannot wait until I do not have to go through these extra steps. I head towards StarDunks before work. I order a coffee, a grilled cheese sandwich and a muffin. I sit down to eat it and it tastes good but not as good as the food in Egypt. After I finish, I head to the food store really quick and buy some things to take back to my abode so that I do not have to eat the government food pellets ever again. I change back into my uniform and again shake my head at this extra step of changing clothes. I take the food and the clothes back to my abode and go to work.

Thanks to the coffee, I feel pretty good today. It will be nice to start every day with a cup of coffee and not have to hide it like this. I also have the meeting set up with my private client today after work. I think it is going to be a good day. Before my trip, I started dreading just going into work. I am glad I got the chance to take my trip and rejuvenate my love for this job. Because in the end, whether I do my job here or there, I want to be a retrieval agent. I like finding the object, it is like knowing that you have successfully solved the puzzle and here is your reward.

The excitable girl comes up to me as soon as I get into the office, again. She asks if I can just walk her through one of my retrieval trips from start to finish. Sure, I can do that. I do not have too many open cases so we go get a hard case from the section of cases that no one can solve. She looks worried. I say do not worry, this is where I usually pick up new cases.

We start the calculations and I tell her that I found this new way of doing the calculations. If she wants to learn from me how I work a case from start to finish, then it should start with me showing her these calculations. I explain how I just thought the calculations could have been better and how I was frustrated when I would go out on a trip and have to look around for the object. I go through the old way and then show her the new way. I show her how much of a difference there is in the results of the two calculations. It is nice to explain this to someone who understands my frustration and can see how beneficial this new way is. The people in Egypt were also appreciative of this new way. So, we get the GPS coordinates and we grab the equipment we will need and we head out in her flying apparatus. We fly to the location and I show her where the two different calculations would have led us. I mark each spot and we search both areas. Of course, what we are looking for is closer to the coordinates using my new method. She is looking at the two marked spots and smiling. I say, I know, it is pretty great to be more accurate. She says with this new info, she could help so many people in our department.

We are looking for things that are tools in a kitchen and I have no idea why the government would want the objects from this location. From what I have read, almost every place that the ancestors lived whether it was in a house, apartment or whatever, almost everyone had kitchen things. But since it seems that I do not understand why the government does anything these days, we start retrieving our items. We grab a couple of examples of silverware, forks, spoons, and knives. In this little area with the silverware, there are plenty of other utensils. I clean off a larger spoon and it has holes in it. Well, that makes no sense. I tell my excitable friend that the ancestors had some funny objects. I motion scooping some dirt with this spoon and some dirt falls through the holes. What is the point of this? We also grab some mugs because they survived and some matching plates. We try to be careful because we do not want to break any of these items once we have found them. We keep searching and also find some pots and pans. I think this is sufficient for what was asked of us. I ask my excitable friend is she wants to keep digging for treasures of her own. She does not because she does not want to keep any treasures at her abode. For as alike as I thought we might be, we are still very different. However, at this point in time, I actually do not want to collect any more treasures either.

While we are out here and no one else is around, I asked her why she seemed to be talking so much the other day. Everyone else in the department seems subdued compared to her. She looks at me, tilts her head a little as if deciding whether to tell me something or not. I tell her that it seems like she had a coffee because that is how I felt after one of my first coffees. Yes! She says, is it obvious because she does not want to get in trouble. Well, I noticed it but I do not think the rest of our coworkers did. I ask her where she went and how she found it. She starts describing StarDunks and says that she was walking into her abode one night and there was someone not in uniform who had something in their hand. She simply went up to them and started asking questions. She ended up trying some of their coffee and she really liked it. Since then she has been going every day for coffee but she has not tried the food yet but she thinks she wants to soon. She also wants to look for the clothes because she is so tired of wearing the same thing every day.

This is perfect, I have been thinking about who could replace me as the carrier and I think she will be interested in it. I tell her that she does have to be careful who she talks to about it but that I will take her there and help her find her first food and then we can go find some clothes. She starts jumping up and down.

Okay but wait a minute, there is something I have to tell you. The government has been putting something in the food pellets to put everyone in a sedated state so she has to calm down a little or someone else will notice. It is okay to be excited but just not at the office. Also, there is some other stuff I can show her and things I can tell her but she has to start keeping secrets. She gives me this huge smile. She says, I am so happy to find someone else to talk to. She says that for the past couple of days everyone she tries talking to just walks away from her. I explain that it is the brain fog that makes everyone seem like they are sleep walking. The more you eat the pellets the more it seems like you just do not seem to notice what is going on around you. I also think that the government might give different food pellets to different people. I do not know how it works but I have also noticed that some people seem more aware than others. It also seems like the longer you eat the pellets, the more of a haze you are in. I think that I stopped being as hazy as the others when I started skipping dinner food pellets.

We finish up with the form and I tell her that I have somewhere to go tonight but tomorrow after work, I will take her to find some real food. We return to the office and I remind her to act like everyone else in the office and to keep her secrets.

When I leave for the day, I go back to my abode and drop off the food and pick up my client's Egyptian glass. I grab my clothes and go to StarDunks. I order some pizza and a cold tea and then wait for my client. I decide not to have any coffee this late in the day. One time I had a coffee late in the afternoon and had a hard time falling asleep that night. When my client arrives, I notice that the color of his skin is very similar to those of the people I met in Egypt. He asks how my trip was and I say that it was very eye opening. I found what he sent me to find. He asks me what I thought about how the government works over there. I tell him that again it was very eye opening and that while it was a very good experience for me, I was also able to help their retrieval department. I ask him where he is from and is it a coincidence that he resembles the people in that country. Oh no, he says, you are correct, I am from Egypt. I have found a way into this country and I am trying to find some resources outside of the city that I think survived the Great War. I found this map and there are some important items marked on it. He was hoping that I could find them for him. He has found a way into the city but has not found a way back out of the city to go look for these things himself. I apologize and say that after my trip to Egypt, I have decided to return there shortly and not come back here. After seeing how much better it is in another country, I can not live under the strict rule of this government. He says he understands. I also tell him that I am training someone to replace me and maybe she will be able to help him in the future. I will contact him if I think she will be interested. He gives me the payment and says that he is happy for me to be able to find happiness in his country. Then he leaves.

I also see a couple of people I have met and tell them that I will be leaving soon but am starting to train a replacement. They ask if I am headed to the community to live and I explain that I am still working out the plans but when I know more, I will tell them. I do not want to jeopardize my exit plan by telling the wrong people. It is hard to know who you can trust even if they are at StarDunks.

The next day before I go to work, I go through my exit plan again. It is all in my head and I find that it is helpful to think about it so that I can stay on track. I have a few things that I have to accomplish but I am glad that I think I have found a replacement to be the carrier. I just have to work with her a little bit more to get her ready to know how to retrieve objects that are for the private clients, how to get in and out of the city when you are not on a work trip, and I have to take her out to the community to introduce her to my mentor.

I arrive at work and start looking for a case to continue to train my replacement with. She comes in and is not as wild as she has been. That is good to see. I tell her that I would like to work together on this case today and she looks like she is half sleeping. Maybe that is not so good. She says that when she went to eat her food pellets last night, there were a couple of red ones mixed in with her nightly meal. That is okay, I tell her, let's just start working through these calculations and she will feel better soon.

This is disturbing because I have heard from some people at StarDunks that once they stopped eating the food pellets, red pellets started showing up in their portions. I think they must have extra sedation additives in them. We start working through this new case and soon we are ready to go find it. The sedation is wearing off little by little. Without looking obvious, I try looking around the office to see who is watching her. Someone in this department must have noticed how excitable she was, but who was it, was it a coworker, or a supervisor or a boss. I have thought before that the other unidentified government agency that I came across might also have some kind of workers that check up on us. I have noticed that every once in a while, there is a new employee who comes into our department who does not work on any cases and then leaves shortly after joining. I did not mention it to anyone because I did not want to call attention to myself.

Before we leave, one of the supervisors that I do not know very well comes up and asks what we are working on. He says that he noticed we are working together and asks if we need some assistance. I think it is this guy because who else would "notice" that? No one has ever approached me before asking if I need assistance. I lie and say that this case was one of the hard ones and when I was away on my trip, no one was working on the hard cases so I thought I would help train other coworkers so everyone would know how to work on these hard cases. He asks me which case I have and I show him the file. He says that he had tried to figure this one out himself but could not. He seems satisfied with my answer and returns to his office.

My excitable coworker and I leave but take my flying apparatus because she still seems too sedated to fly. I stop by StarDunks and go inside quickly and get her a vanilla latte. When I return and hand her the drink, she finally starts to smile. Try this one, I like it. She takes a sip and we head towards the location. She finally starts coming around and I tell her that today is not about the retrieval mission that I have a lot to tell her.

First of all, she has to stop eating the food pellets and definitely has to stay away from that supervisor that stopped us on the way out. She says she feels better now that she has the coffee, but she sees how the food pellets made her feel like she was asleep. I explain that I do not understand all of it but I want to tell her what I know, but maybe not everything I know. I am still unsure what to do with the information that I found about our country starting the Great War and I cannot tell her that. So I start with my warning again that she has to be careful who she talks to. I tell her that I am going to show her real food and clothes. I am going to introduce her to some people who want to leave the city and I am going to show her how to find the community of people living outside of the city. She just looks at me and asks how people can live outside of the city. I gesture with my arms, we are outside the city, does it look as dangerous to her like the government says it is in their advertisements? She looks around. No, for as many times as she has been out here, she has never felt in danger. The government lies, I tell her. After the first time she had the coffee, did she die? No, she laughs, I am not dead. The government lies, I tell her. There are some people who have found a way to live outside the city because they just can not live under the strict rules and the lies from the government. And one of the main leaders in this community was the person who was my mentor when I first came to the department. She is one of us.

She asks me when I started having doubts about the government and how did I find all of this out. She says that she never knew any of this and probably never thought about it before. I get up and hug her. I want her to think for herself and am glad she asked. I have been having doubts for a while and it started on my first trip outside of the city when I saw that it was not as dangerous as the government advertisements made it out to be. After that little things just did not make any sense, like how there were repeat customers at StarDunks who did not die after eating non-government food that was not the food pellets. I have kept everything quiet because I do not know what would happen if the government found out about the community or about StarDunks. And I do not know what happens to people like me who do not believe everything that the government says. Which is why I keep warning her not to call any attention to herself. I really do not think any of our coworkers have any of the doubts about the government that I do. They are like her, they go to work, do their job and just live their life.

She says that she is excited to learn more. She has noticed that some of our coworkers seemed to be in a haze and wondered why they were like that. She has often wondered why she was the only one who would get excited about the finds. She thought she was the only one who wondered some of these things. I tell her that at the motel site, when she found the statue, I had already found one and I have a treasure room at my abode for things I take home from retrieval sites. Can I see them, she asks. Absolutely, I would love to share my treasures with someone who will appreciate them as much as I do. I explain a few more things and tell her that when we go to StarDunks I am going to introduce her as the new carrier.

We leave and head back to my abode so I can grab my other clothes. I show her some of my treasures. She really likes my rings and I think she will like the radio, so I turn it on and tune into my favorite station. She looks at me, looks at the radio and I start dancing around. She starts giggling. How did I ever find this? I do not know. I just come across things and then I research them and kind of go from there. She looks really happy, but I tell her she has to learn when it is okay to be happy and when she has to be serious and look sedated. So we act sedated and leave my abode. We get to the parking spot and I show her where I am going to change my clothes. We walk in and I order her a grilled cheese sandwich and a doughnut. I get a spinach quiche. We sit down and I tell her that she should try the grilled cheese sandwich first. She takes a bite and her face lights up, this is amazing, she says. I know, right? I ordered an apple juice and an orange juice. I tell her there are more things to drink than just coffee. I give her a bite of my quiche. Then I tell her to try the doughnut. She is so amazed. I tell her I felt the same way! We finish our meal and then we head to the clothing store. This was not my favorite place and I really felt overwhelmed when I first came here, but not this girl. She is looking at all the fabrics, she wants to touch all the clothes. She holds them up and twirls around. The girl working at this store comes up and they start talking about which fabrics feel better than others. She grabs a couple of outfits and tries them on. She comes out and says "you have got to see this!" She is as excited about these clothes as I get about food. I tell her to buy what she wants but that she has to come and go in her uniform so she does not attract any more attention to herself. I tell her she can change into these clothes and wear them here or in her abode.

We head to the food store next and I explain that if she keeps some food at her abode, she does not have to eat any more of the food pellets. And after a while she will not need the coffee to wake her up for the hazy feeling the food pellets make her feel. Actually, she should probably not drink too much coffee because it really does make her pretty wild. We leave this store and I show her a couple of others. I tell her she can explore the rest of them on her own.

I feel pretty confident that she will make a good replacement. I do not want to attract too much more attention so I tell her to work on her own for a couple of days and then I will show her more soon.

The next day at work I try to find a case that will take me in the direction of the history museum. I go into the archives and check the information about this history museum. There is more information missing than the last time I checked. I am not sure why the government wants to suppress this information. What harm does it do to let the people know what their real history is? I head out of the office and fly towards the first museum. I park and make sure no one is following me. I then walk around a few buildings and come to the one where I hid the war files. I grab them and hurry back to my flying apparatus. As I am flying back towards the city, I notice that there is another flying apparatus headed towards me. I alter my flight plan because this other apparatus looks like they are headed right towards me. I see that it is one of the agents from the unidentified government agency that I encountered before. It is not the same guard but he has the same uniform. I turn around a couple times and he lands at the museum that I just left. I think that I better start being more careful where I go. I am not sure why the government is taking more notice of what I am doing but with that and the fact that more information is missing from the archives, it is starting to make me nervous. I head straight back to my abode and hide the file in my treasure room. Then I go back to the office. I put my head down and work hard the rest of the day. That night I go through my exit plan again. I might need to change the timeline a little.

I go to work the next day with the intention of sitting at my desk all day so I do not attract any more attention. I work at updating the archives from any of the cases I have closed but did not have the time to finish them completely. Once I save the information, it says that once verification has taken place, the information will be added. That is a new step. I wonder who does this new verifying step. At this point I do not want to start asking questions because I just want to keep my head down and finish out the rest of my exit plan. Everything seems to be okay today. I go back to my abode after work and stay there all night. I make myself some dinner from the food I bought from the food store. I go through my food pellets and do not find any red pellets. I wonder why the excitable girl had red pellets already and I never received any. I go through the treasures in my treasure room and decide which ones I want to keep and which ones I need to move out of here. Once I leave, they, whoever they may be, will go through my abode looking for clues to where and why I left. I have to leave absolutely no clues. I think the only thing that I want to pass on is my radio, other than that, I can take my treasures into StarDunks and let others have them.

I wake up the next day and have a lot of different tasks I need to do today. I start by packing up my treasures and going to StarDunks. I get a coffee and leave my box in a booth for anyone to take whatever it is they want. I tell them that I will be back later today. I go to work, grab a case file and head out again. I fly to the replica city and go to the treasure room that one of my clients sent me to. I grab a couple of containers of cash, coins and jewels. I quickly load it into my flying apparatus then fly to the next building. Again, I grab a couple of containers of cash and jewels. I decide not to grab the ones with coins because they seem pretty heavy. I load those containers and fly to the museum that I found here, just in case I was followed again. I park my flying apparatus in a spot that cannot be seen from the air. I can hear another flying transport coming and I crouch down so that they cannot see me either. They fly towards the building I went to first. While I am crouched down, I see a red blinking light on my flying apparatus. I did not see that before. I go over and pull it off of my apparatus and there is what looks like a switch on it. I move the switch and the light goes off. I wonder if this has any connection to being followed. I am not sure what it is but I think I need to get out of this city and start on my trip back. As long as it is off, I convince myself on the trip back that maybe I need to drop these containers off somewhere before I enter the city again. I fly in this direction and I fly in that direction so if the other flying apparatus happens to have caught up with me, they will not know where I am heading. I look behind me a couple of times and do not see him. I fly over a spot where I have been on a trip before and decide that I will remember how to find this place so I land. I find a hiding place for the containers and leave again.

This time I fly to my abode, grab some clothes and my secret government file and head to StarDunks. When I park, I crouch down to see if any other flying apparatuses have this red blinking light on and a couple of them do. I switch them off and walk inside. When I walk in, I say loudly, I think the government is looking for this place. I have found these little boxes on a couple of the flying apparatuses outside and I want to show everyone what to look for. We go outside and I show them which ones they were on and show them how to turn them off. I also tell them that I was just followed by an employee wearing a uniform that I did not recognize, so please be careful. A couple of them look at each other and start talking. They tell me that if this is how far the government has gone to control them, then they are ready to leave. I think that is a great idea. I tell them to go to their abode and get what they need, bring their unused food pellets and to meet me here in an hour.

I return to work and find my excitable coworker. She smiles discreetly at me and I tell her things have changed and I have to show her something. We go to her flying apparatus and I show her how to turn off the red blinking light. I tell her that I was followed on my last two trips and that some of the people at StarDunks had these devices on their apparatuses also. I tell her that I have to show her how to get these people out of the city and then I am leaving. I have one more trip to make but she needs to meet me at StarDunks in a half an hour.

I go back to my abode and grab everything that I need. I then return to the spot where I hid the containers. I grab them and then go to StarDunks just in time to meet the people who are ready to leave. My excitable friend arrives and I check again that there are no new red light devices.

EXODUS

We head out of the city in the safest direction I know because this time there is a large group of flying apparatuses and that is not a common sight. We fly out fast and in the wrong direction. We fly out until I know we can not be seen by anyone in the city and then head towards another wrong direction for a while. We start heading towards the community and I know this might scare my mentor but I am sure she will understand once I explain what is happening. We land and I tell everyone to stay where they are until I come back. I run to go meet my mentor and my new friend. I apologize for bringing so many people in their flying apparatuses but things have gotten worse in the city. My mentor says that is why she left, when things got worse for her. She says she is ready to welcome everyone and we walk back to the group together. I keep talking to my mentor as my new friend welcomes everyone and tells them where to go, what to do and where to park their flying apparatuses. I introduce my excitable friend to my mentor and tell her that she must be really careful coming and going back and forth to the city. If she has any questions, she will have to ask my mentor going forward. She says it will be a great adventure. Perfect!

I tell my mentor that I have come across an unidentified government agency a couple of times, once while they were following me and once because I think I found something they were looking for. I tell her that our country started the Great War and I have proof of it. I do not know what to do with the proof and I am leaving the country shortly to go back to Egypt and live there. I tell her I think the information would be the safest with her and I give her the file. I also tell her that I found something of value and I also want to give her that as well. I give her some of the containers of jewels, all of the coins and some of the cash. I tell her that I told the others to bring their food pellets in case they could use them. The last thing I hand her is the coordinates for the underground storage and tell her how to find the storage that contained the food. I explain that since they have plenty of flying apparatuses now, they might be able to go there and get more food. Although she would be the most qualified to fly there.

She smiles and says that she did not even know how valuable I would be to her when she picked me to mentor. She says that they use the food pellets to help make the food grow from the ground. She knows there will be use for the jewels and the coins because she has found some trading partners that she can exchange them for animals or more food. But she says she also does not know what to do with the government information about the war. She asks me how I found it. I tell her about the replica city and finding the ancestors' museums. Then on another trip to a different museum I just happened to walk into a government office building and I found them. After I read them, I knew how important they would be but I did not know until I saw the other government agents just how important they would be.

She then asks me why I was leaving the country. I could just live with them. I tell her that in this other country, I could still do my job, which I do still love, but that life was so much better there. If I did not love my job so much, I would live here in the community with them, but there is still excitement for me in finding an object and seeing how it played a role in history. And I really like the fact that when you suggest a change, this other government will actually consider it. There are so many things I like about the food and the dancing and the clothes there. She understands. She tells me that she heard that our country used to be like that before also but it is getting worse all the time. I thank her for picking me to mentor and all for the lessons that she taught me. I give her a big hug and say goodbye.

I get back into my flying apparatus and leave to fly back to Egypt. I am so excited to finally be leaving but I find that I am sad to leave some of these great people behind. The trip seems longer this time because it is dark when I leave. I have the coordinates programmed into my flying apparatus so I leave the majority of the flying up to the machine. I think through my exit plan. The only thing that was on my list that I did not have time for was to go collect those other government secrets that I found and hid in the underground storage facility. Well I know where I put them in case I ever need to go get them. I also think that if I ever need to, I can always go to the replica city and find more treasure.

Because it is dark out, I cannot see any of the ocean animals. But I look at the stars above and the farther away from the Apple I am, the stress leaves and the happiness returns. I am looking forward to this new life.

I arrive in Egypt and head to the retrieval department. I walk in and say hello to the security guard. He again walks me into the retrieval department because I do not have a badge to get through the secure doors. I walk in and everyone is happy to see me. My contact is not there, a coworker says that he is out on a mission and he will be back soon. I go talk to the supervisor and ask if I can have a job working in this department. Absolutely! She starts all of the processes and assigns me to the vacant abode that I had stayed in while I was here before. I tell her that it was a long trip and I am tired. I ask if I can go rest and come in tomorrow to start to work. She agrees and says that when I come in tomorrow, she will have everything ready for me. She looks at me and says, we are really happy that you came back to us but why so soon? I say that things had changed and I will explain tomorrow. I leave to go to the vacant abode and fall asleep as soon as I lie down. I have the best dreams about food and I wake up hungry. I look and find that the food is still here. I make myself something to eat and feel immediately better.

The next day, I go into work and start living the life that I love every part of. I make some great friends in my department. I go on amazing retrieval trips and feel really valued for the work that I do. And the best part of all is that my love for my job has returned. I look forward to going to work every day. My contact takes me to other countries on work trips to collaborate with them. And of course, we try new food everywhere we go. I think about my mentor, my new friend and my excitable friend from time to time and hope everything is still good for them.

I have traveled to many different countries around the world and seen how the Great War affected my country the most. But I also learned from other countries that my country bombed some of its own cities to rally the citizens. That makes sense with what I have seen, how there was so much different damage to different parts of the country. Bombs in one city did not have the same effect as the bombs did in another city. I have slowly been working through the containers of jewels and cash that I brought with me. I still think that if I need to go back, I know where to get more but I do not necessarily need it. I have thought about if I were to go back, who would I give it to. But for now, I am so happy with where I am that I do not want to go back, not even for more treasure.

Made in the USA
Monee, IL
31 May 2021